BINDING
THE
BARONESS

CAVERN OF PLEASURES

BESTSELLING AUTHOR
EM BROWN

BINDING
THE
BARONESS

CHAPTER ONE

T EN THOUSAND POUNDS if you will seduce the Baroness
Debarlow."

Montague Edwards eyed the Earl of Frotham without evincing
emotion though he could have choked on the snuff he had just inhaled.
Ten thousand pounds. The sum reverberated gloriously in his ears. The
invitation from Frotham had come as surprise enough for Montague
barely knew the Earl and his family. The aforementioned proposition
was beyond expectation. The old man, frowning from behind his large
mahogany writing table, appeared not to be jesting, if such a jest fell
within the inclinations of the Earl—which Montague doubted.

Without word, Montague took another pinch of snuff and replaced
his snuffbox into his waistcoat pocket. He should have leaped without
question at such an opportunity, but he wanted time to quiet his
excitement. How often did one come across ten thousand pounds? He
had come to London, despite his aversion to The Season, to seek that
which he had never craved or thought he needed: a wife. To be precise,
he needed funds. A wife, with the proper endowment, was simply a
means to that end.

"Five and ten then," the Earl, mistaking Montague's silence,
amended.

The man was desperate, Montague surmised as he noted his
surroundings. The silk-lined walls of the library, the stately furnishings,
and paintings mounted in gilded frames all suggested Frotham had the
means to make such an offer, but appearances could deceive. Clearly
something important was at stake for Frotham to state such an

outlandish proposal. Montague wondered what it could be. His dispassion appeared to rankle the Earl, who tried unsuccessfully to suppress the irritation from his voice.

"Are you not in need of five and ten thousand pounds, sir?" Frotham asked. "Many a young man of standing would want years to generate such income. One could do much with such an amount."

Only a fool would not recognize that fact, Montague thought wryly, but he had no wish to offend the Earl into withdrawing the proposition at hand. Instead, Montague responded, "You mistake my years. I am hardly deemed callow with four and thirty years to my name."

"Shall we agree it be no paltry sum for any man?"

"Indeed. Are you so desirous then to part with it?"

Frotham had a pronounced jaw, and it jutted out with displeasure. He might have presented a handsome man in his youth, but a rich diet had made his jowls more prominent, and his constant battle with the gout had rendered his countenance surly.

"I understand you are short in the way of funds," the Earl countered.

Montague stiffened. Choosing not to respond immediately to such a pointed statement, he took a seat on the richly upholstered settee. Crossing one leg over the other, he studied his shoes. He had spent more than he ought to have on his pair of silver buckles, but he could not expect to entice a woman of wealth without the proper attire. Five and ten thousand pounds could buy a great number of buckles. It was enough to save Chelton. It would eliminate the need to marry.

"And that is why you have chosen me to receive your generous offer?" Montague asked, calmly raising a brow.

He was met with a tight smile.

"The reputation you have in Bath precedes you, sir," Frotham answered. "I am familiar with your…conquests, shall we say?"

Frotham's frown and humorless eyes indicated the statement was not intended as flattery. Montague suspected he was not favored by the Earl, but that mattered not.

"And you wish me to apply myself to this Baroness Debarlow.

Why?"

Frotham shifted uncomfortably. "That is my concern. Yours is the ten thousand pounds should you prove successful."

"Five and ten," Montague corrected. "And what shall be considered a mark of success where the Baroness is concerned? Is it sufficient that I bed her once? Twice?"

"You can bed her as often as you like," Frotham bristled.

"Or as little? The Baroness Debarlow must be homely indeed to require five and ten thousand pounds as recompense."

"There are many who would consider her pleasing to the eye, though she has not half the refinement of features as her...You will find her comely enough, I assure you."

"Then what, pray, is her flaw?" Montague baited. He had been tempted to accept the Earl's proposal without question, but desperate as he was for the funds, he would not throw all caution to wind. "She is odious in some form, is she not?"

"Not in any way that would deter the likes of you."

Montague raised a brow. "My partialities are familiar to you?"

"Is it not a sport for men of your sort? I should hardly have to compensate you for the effort," scoffed Frotham, no longer able to contain his disdain.

"Then you must be distressed indeed."

Unaccustomed to being denied and with such flippancy, the Earl growled, "Do we have a deal, sir?"

Rising to his feet, Montague decided to put an end to their *tete-a-tete*. "The terms are such: you will pay an advance of five thousand pounds, and *twenty* thousand upon completion of the charge. I will know the situation prompting this commission. If the intent is to cuckold the Baron Debarlow and incite him into challenging me to a duel, I shall have to request a greater sum an I am to risk my head being blown off."

Montague watched as Frotham turned all shades of red, finally settling on a hue not unlike that of a fresh cut of raw beefsteak. For a moment, Montague wondered if he had overplayed his hand.

"The Baroness is a widow," said Frotham through clenched teeth.

"And I shall not agree to such outrageous terms."

"Then I bid you have a good evening, my lord." Montague bowed his head and turned toward the door.

The Earl made a series of grunting sounds before saying, "If you please..."

Montague stayed his hand upon the door handle.

"Very well. I accept your terms."

Montague breathed a private sigh of relief before turning to the Earl.

"But you will have a month to succeed or fail," Frotham said. "You will observe the utmost discretion. If anyone were to gain awareness of this matter, our arrangement is forfeit."

"You have my confidence."

Frotham did not appear comforted and gnawed his words as if fearful his teeth would fall out during his speech. "She has ensnared my son."

"The Viscount Tremayne?"

"He is to wed Elisabeth Worsely. Her father and I have agreed it is a most suitable match, but Charles will not offer for her hand while he is smitten with the Baroness. I have enticed and threatened him in as many ways, but not even the threat of poverty will dissuade him from her."

"Perhaps he perceives it an empty threat," Montague offered, "as it would only augment that which you seek to avoid."

Frotham nodded. "His *association* with the Baroness is scandalous enough. She has at least thirty years to her name and he but two and twenty. There are many women of far greater beauty and charm than she, but Charles follows her about like a wretched pup to its master's heel. She has no breeding, and it astounds me still how someone as common as she could have married the Baron Debarlow. Her motives of greed were obvious, and he has left her a grand fortune upon his death."

"Are you so sure it not be a passing fancy between your son and Lady Debarlow?"

"It were as if she had powers of sorcery over him. I fear he would wed the Baronness if naught be done."

Tremayne was the only son and heir for the Earl, whose only other child was a younger daughter. Marriage to Debarlow would be disastrous for Frotham.

"And I am to woo the Baroness from your son, freeing him to marry Miss Worsely," Montague concluded.

"Precisely. My son must never know of our arrangement."

"Where can I introduce myself to the Baroness?"

"There is to be a ball given by Lord and Lady Bennington a fortnight hence. I shall arrange to have you as a guest of my friend Mr. Henry who will be in attendance."

CHAPTER TWO

THE VISCOUNT TREMAYNE strained against the bindings that secured him to the wooden cross behind him. Every shred of clothing had been stripped from him, leaving him as naked as a babe newborn to the world. He shut his eyes that he might not know if the other patrons of Madame Botreaux's *Cavern of Pleasures* could see him thus, bound, exposed, and helpless. Those that came to the secret underground assembly observed a code of silence respecting the identities of their fellow patrons. The slightest slip of the tongue ensured a swift expulsion from the *Cavern*. Nevertheless, many wore masks to preserve their anonymity. But his mask lay upon the ground at *her* feet, taunting him with its uselessness. He, the Viscount Tremayne, future Earl of Frotham, was bared for all to see. The darkness of the lair, illuminated by candelabras placed sufficiently far in corners to cast the scantest of light, provided no comfort. Shame colored his cheeks even as a peculiar thrill ran hot through his veins, churning in his groin, and pulsing in his cock.

In stark contrast to his nudity, the Baroness Debarlow stood in full dress and mask. Even her bronze colored hair was concealed beneath powder. He marveled at her beauty. Long ivory gloves encased firm yet supple arms. Hers were not the scrawny limbs of the younger chits who vied for his attention. Her full bosom curved lusciously above her corset. Her pale unblemished skin glowed with a luster that no rouge could engender. Though her shoulders lacked the dramatic slope defined by the standards of current feminine beauty, he would have given much to kiss that part of her. Even her height—she stood as tall as he when in her heels—did not dissuade him.

With a quick flick of her forearm, Abigail Debarlow landed the cat-o-nine tails across his chest. He grimaced but she knew he reveled in the pain. Deep within her, simmering embers of a fervor threatening to burst into flame compelled her to lash him with greater vigor, but she stayed the desire, not wishing to frighten him. She had labored far too hard cultivating his devotion to risk any setbacks. With his breeding and handsome features, he could command the attention of women far younger and comelier than she. The older women doted on his *fine* brown eyes with their large bright irises. The younger women admired his form, which he kept lean through a healthy allowance of sport.

Perhaps it was her easy dismissal of him upon their initial meeting that roused his attention for undoubtedly the young Viscount was wont to be the recipient of greater attention, especially among the fair sex.

* * * * *

"She is beautiful."

The wake of the dashing mare swept the words from his mouth and the breath from his breast. Charles had never seen such a splendid specimen of an Arabian. She galloped smoothly along the fence, appearing as if she might take flight at any moment. The movement of her muscles mesmerized him even more than her gleaming coat of black. Though his father would oppose adding another horse to his stable, Charles could not resist the gasps of admiration that were sure to follow when he unveiled this prize at the races.

"I will take her," Charles pronounced, barely able to contain his grin, to the shorter man beside him. "You have outdone yourself, O'Kearney. By far, you can claim to breed the best horses this side of the Thames."

O'Kearney, scratching his neck, looked away. "I thank ye for yar kind words, m'lord. But I fear she be taken."

Charles could not believe it. This horse was meant to be his. "Taken? By whom?"

"By me."

He turned and beheld a woman in a blue riding habit donning a pair of white riding gloves. From the tailoring of the jacket, which molded her body most impressively, and the sharp cravat at her throat, he discerned her to be a woman of quality. The first blossom of youth had passed the peak of bloom for her, but she was no less striking. Charles felt a sense of relief. A woman would be easier to persuade. And one with a few more years of maturity. He found the younger, prettier ones could possess the most unappealing haughtiness, expecting that even men of distinction should treat them as if they were crowned princesses.

"You are a fine judge of horseflesh, madam," he praised with a step towards her. "Allow me to introduce myself. I am the Viscount Tremayne."

He doffed his hat and bowed, but when he met her gaze again, he did not perceive any glint of interest in her greyish blue eyes. She looked him over with what seemed to be tedium or even disdain. He would have dismissed her as unperceptive or of a cantankerous disposition, but she possessed something he desired. He had no choice but to engage.

"And you are?" he prompted with his most charming smile when it became clear she was not to offer her name. He decided she was both unperceptive *and* cantankerous.

"Baroness Debarlow," she tossed over her shoulder as she went to stand at the fence to watch the mare.

Well, Charles thought to himself, *appearances can deceive.* He had never met Lady Debarlow before, but he knew the scandal of her marriage to the late Baron Debarlow. With his wealth, the Baron could have chosen from any number of willing women, but he elected a most common woman. She must possess extraordinary powers of seduction, Charles concluded, to have ensnared one of the most eligible bachelors. He wondered what manner of tricks she engaged in the bedchambers to have won the Baron over.

She raised an elegantly arched brow at him, and he realized he was grinning at the thought of her naked in bed.

He cleared his throat. "My condolences on the passing of your husband, my lady."

"His death amuses you?"

"No, I…"

His cheeks grew warm. He was near to disliking this woman. Perhaps she was not so comely. She had not applied enough powder to conceal the darker tint of her complexion, bronzed perhaps by hours riding in the sun. Nevertheless, one who did not possess skin of alabaster should, at the least, employ the cosmetic arts to her advantage. And yet, she did possess a regal carriage unexpected in one given her circumstances. No doubt it was an effort to mask an ordinary origin.

"The Baron was much respected," he said.

She looked him over before turning her attention back to the mare. "You are young to have known him well."

He bristled. Did she think him an adolescent? Perhaps it was best to change the subject of discussion. He followed her gaze.

"A magnificent mare, is she not?"

She said nothing.

"And an impressive gait."

Still nothing.

He decided a polite *tete-a-tete* would not be possible with this woman. He might as well come forth with his intentions.

"I would buy her from you."

"A bad temperament has the horse," O'Kearney warned. "Terrible skittish."

"I have no interest in selling her." She turned to O'Kearney. "Saddle her, if you would."

"But you have yet to hear my price," Charles pressed.

"I have no interest in your money."

"I will pay you double for the mare."

That gave her pause. She turned to look at him. "I paid two hundred pounds."

Charles blanched. Perhaps it was just as well she was not interested in selling. He had not four hundred pounds—not without pleading before his father, who was not likely to approve the purchase. The chorus of admiration and envy he was expecting to hear from his peers began to fade into a mere dream.

Distressed, he blurted, "I would have thought the sum of four hundred pounds could merit your attention."

She had been watching O'Kearney struggling to cinch the saddle about the mare but now she turned to him with narrowed eyes. "You had not heard, perhaps, the claims that I married the Baron for his wealth. Having accomplished such a feat, I have no need for *your* money."

She left him at a loss for words. It was not often that he felt like a fool. The sensation was most uncomfortable.

The Baroness walked over to the mare and placed a firm hand upon the horse. He could not hear the words she spoke, but the mare calmed enough for O'Kearney to put the reins over the horse.

"Allow me," Charles said, springing forward when he saw O'Kearney about to assist the Baroness. Putting his gloved hands together, he formed a bridge for her to step on. He hoisted her onto the horse. Stepping back, he admired the vision before him. The mare pranced in place but showed no other signs of a flawed disposition. It was evident from the ease with which the Baroness held the reins while maintaining her tall posture that she was an experienced horsewoman. Perhaps she was not so plain in features. Astride a horse, she presented a compelling vision. His interest turned from the horse to its rider. No woman had ever denied Tremayne before, and neither would Lady Debarlow.

* * * * *

"I trust you will not make the same error at the Bennington ball?" Abigail asked of Charles as she surveyed the series of bright pink marks she had left across his chest, thighs and arms with her lash. His cock stood at rigid attention, his body trembling for release. But she would not allow it. He had wronged her at the last assembly, embarrassed her among the quidnuncs eager to discuss when the Viscount would finally tire of her in favor of younger, prettier women.

"I will dance with none other lest I have first danced with you," he said.

"Invited me to dance," she corrected. "Whether I shall accept is a different matter."

He winced. Walking over to where he stood still pinioned to the post, she released his bonds. He fell to his knees and kissed the laces upon her boot.

"Forgive me, Mistress."

She smiled. "You are forgiven."

"My lady is most merciful. Your benevolence is the greatest honor. I am unworthy of your forbearance. You—"

"Enough."

She had been willing enough to play the role of mistress to him, but his excessive flattery was most tedious.

"You may apply twenty lashes to your back so that you may fortify your lesson," she added, dropping the lash where he knelt.

He bowed. "Thank you, Mistress."

She walked out of the alcove to the sound of the lash falling against his body. She shook off the sensations of guilt that always crawled upon her since the day her lash had first fallen upon him. He deserved worse than she gave. She would spit upon the name of Frotham for what they had done to her family. Fate had been cruel, but that capricious goddess had seen fit to present this most unusual opportunity to avenge the wrong. She knew the Earl to suffer great consternation over his son's infatuation with her. He would be appalled if he knew that his son patronized Madame Botreaux's *Cavern of Pleasures*, but he would not disown his only son and heir to the earldom.

Unless the Viscount chose to marry her.

Such a prospect was not entirely improbable if she played her cards with care. Even then, the dismay of the Earl could not compare— indeed, it would pale beside all that her mother had suffered. When she closed her eyes, the image of her mother's decaying body shown bold

11

and bright as if the twenty years since her passing were but yesterday.

Taking a haggard breath, Abigail willed away the memory. She would not brook any weakness in herself. Not now. Not ever.

"I would I were made of stronger mettle," her mother had once despaired shortly before she began her long and arduous road to death.

Abigail had vowed never to echo her mother's lament. She looked about the *Cavern*, a large assembly hall sunken below ground. The main floor was surrounded by alcoves occupied by masked patrons engaging in various forms of bondage. There were Masters and Mistresses of all kinds. In one corner alcove, two masters pleasured a female submissive. In another, a man stripped to the buff knelt before another, paying homage to the large erection protruding before him.

For a moment she studied a Mistress named Lady Athena, a young woman who wielded the crop like no other. But Abigail did not aspire to be the most dominant Mistress despite the ease with which she had adopted her role with Charles. In truth, she much preferred to be the woman bent and bound over the back of the chair being pleasured by *him*.

She had heard tales that he might be Vale Montressor Aubrey, the third Marquess of Dunnesford, but he always wore a silver and white mask. Nonetheless, having observed the manner in which Lord Aubrey moved and gauging his height and physique—in particular, the way his breeches and stockings molded his legs—she would have wagered the rumors to be true. Abigail eyed the muscular planes of his chest and ran her tongue over her lower lip. Here was a man, unlike the boy she dabbled with. She watched as Dunnesford brought his submissive to climax by rubbing his crop along her mons. The woman cried out in her ecstasy at length. Abigail wondered the woman had breath enough left in her lungs. She watched as he departed his alcove.

"If you ever wish to have yourself a woman who can match your talents, you have but to call upon me," she said to him as he passed her by.

He stopped slowly in his tracks and looked at her, pinning her to her spot with his stare. Heart thumping, she lifted her chin.

"You have not long been a patron of Madame Botreaux," he noted, "yet have an assessment of my talents."

"I am a quick observer," she replied.

He continued to stare at her. She could not discern what he thought of her, but the fact that he had noticed she was a newer visitor to the *Cavern* was heartening.

"You are brazen," he corrected, "for surely you have been informed of the hierarchy here."

She knew the order at Madame Botreaux's. A junior patron would not initiate a dialogue with a senior dominant.

"Such defiance has consequences," he continued.

She gave him a sly half smile. "I would welcome any punishment you would administer. Strap and bind me as you wish. I should like nothing more than to be bound and whipped at your hand."

"Be careful of what you wish."

After holding her gaze for a prolonged minute, he turned and walked away, up the grand staircase to the balcony where Penelope Botreaux had a view of everyone in the *Cavern*. Only the most distinguished guests were ever invited to the balcony with Madame Botreaux. Abigail drank in the lingering aura of the Marquess and shivered. His tone, devoid of cheer or disdain, had relayed little of how he perceived her advances. One could interpret the intensity of his stare as a warning that she behave herself, but if he had completely disapproved of her, he would have made that known to her.

But he would have to wait for her attention. For now, her aim was the Viscount Tremayne. She intended to hasten her plans with the Viscount, beginning with the Bennington ball. If she succeeded, she would have in hand a proposal of marriage within the month.

CHAPTER THREE

Y OU HAVE ASSEMBLED quite the dossier on the Baroness," remarked Latimer Holmes, putting down the sheafs of paper to watch his friend dress.

Assisted by his valet, Montague shrugged into his coat of olive velvet. Cut by one of the finest tailors of Savile Row, the coat fit about his broad shoulders with every appearance of being too snug while actually allowing movement. The cutaway revealed plenty of the gold embroidered waistcoat and the tight fit of his breeches.

"Twenty thousand pounds be at stake, my friend," Montague reminded as he adjusted his snowy cravat. "I do not take this assignment lightly."

"And you think you can complete the task?"

Montague looked himself in the mirror. With his dark brown hair clubbed smartly at the neck with a bow, not a hair out of place, his pointed shoes polished to shine in the dimmest setting, he felt, at the least, attired for the occasion.

"I have little choice but to succeed," he replied grimly.

"I doubt not your abilities. I still marvel how you managed to bed that Austrian Comtesse. She were as frigid as a Russian winter. I imagine the Baroness to be an easier fox to hunt. Quite bourgeois, you know, baroness or no."

"A woman's pedigree is no indicator of her receptiveness to being seduced."

He glanced over a sheet of paper listing all known lovers of the Baroness Debarlow. There were over a dozen names including the

Viscount Tremayne and the Baron Debarlow—provided she had indeed consummated the marriage. She had been married to the Baron for two years, but Montague knew of husbands and wives who had not coupled for far more years. From what he could discern from sources other than Frotham, the marriage to Debarlow had shocked everyone in polite society. While her motives had been evident, those of the Baron could not be more baffling. Some speculated Debarlow to have had a lapse in reason, though Montague had found no evidence suggesting that the man was not in full possession of his faculties. Others speculated that Abigail had unearthed a dark secret in the Debarlow family and blackmailed him into marriage. No one believed that theirs was a union founded on affection. A few even suggested that the Baron met his early death as result of foul play.

But more consequential to Montague than the views espoused by Frotham's peers were those of the Debarlow servants. His own valet, Jonathan, a young man whose rugged countenance could win over men and women alike, had befriended a number of the maids at the Debarlow estate. Their accounts presented a different portrayal. While the maids did find the marriage rather mysterious, the Baroness was found in the Baron's bed from time to time, or he in hers. The pair frequently went out together. If they parted ways afterwards, it was not plain for they arrived home together. Their servants did not profess there to be love but cited moments of laughter and affection between the two.

"Then what markers do you seek?" asked Latimer as he flared his tailcoats and sat down. "Or do you prefer to say that seducing a woman were more art than science?"

Montague took his gloves and allowed Jonathan to tie his cloak about him. "Your success would be limited if you attempted to formulate principles upon which to base your efforts. Each woman is singular. Each one unique."

"That were a bloody shame. Then you have nothing to teach?"

Montague gave his friend a wry smile through the mirror.

Refusing to relinquish hope, Latimer pursued, "But surely you can form some rubrics to apply to the majority? The older ones, for example, must be easier to seduce. Their beauty waning, they are more apt to long for admiration and the courtship of their youth."

"They are also wiser and more discerning. The young can be tempted by novelty, thrilled by a nascent lust they do not as yet fully comprehend."

"Then a virgin were more easy to seduce."

"It would depend upon her temperament. Fear can be quite the effective guard to a woman's honor."

His friend knit his brows before perking at hopeful attention. "What of the homelier ones? Certainly they would perceive any effort to seduce them as flattery."

"Perhaps. I have been fortunate my experience with that set has been limited."

Latimer grinned at having discovered a positive theory but frowned when he realized he would have no interest in applying the newfound knowledge.

Reading his friend's thoughts, Mongague laughed and put a consoling grip upon Latimer's shoulder. "When you have found a woman to woo, I give you leave to seek my consultation. I have no tenets to impart but may yet be of service."

Heartened, Latimer leaned back in his chair and eyed Montague through his quizzing glass. "I must say you cut a striking figure, Edwards, when in *grand parure*. The Bennington ball is no small affair. Will you attend sans powder?"

"You know I bear no affinity for it." Despite a studious attention to his appearance, he had no tolerance for sitting in a chair to have a hairdresser grease and starch his hair.

"I have mine scented with lavender such that I walk in a garden wherever I roam."

"Perhaps a first lesson in the study of seduction is to scent your powder with *her* preferred fragrance."

"And know you the *parfum* of choice for the Baroness?"

"Orange flower."

The answer came effortlessly enough but as Montague sat in his carriage to the Bennington ball, he wondered that seducing the Baroness would prove as easy. He knew not why, but he felt a rare unease. Perhaps it was the twenty thousand pounds at stake. Perhaps because the information he had collected about Abigail Debarlow did not paint a clear portrait of the woman. Why would a woman of her status favor a young man who seemed so different from her late husband? Was it for her vanity? Was she attempting to recapture her youth? Was the Viscount of such irresistible charms? He would have to know the answers.

* * * * *

Charles descended the wide marble stairs into the foyer, decorated by silk floral garlands and lighted by a gilded chandelier of candles. Perturbed by having had to listen to his aunt lament her various ailments while they waited behind at least twenty carriages before they could alight from their own, he had no eye for his lavish surroundings. His gaze sought only one person. He could hardly wait to show the Baroness his devotion. Their last encounter at Madame Botreaux's had him quaking with fear and reverence at what she might do if he did not follow her directives with the utmost diligence.

"Who is that man standing with Mr. Henry?" asked Evalina, his sister and junior of four years.

He gave a cursory glance at the tall gentleman of dark brown hair. After briefly admiring the cut of the man's coat, he returned to searching for the Baroness.

"I know not," he mumbled as he veered to the left. Perhaps the Baroness awaited in the gardens. In his blue silk coat, rose colored waistcoat, and embroidered stockings, he expected Abigail to be taken by him.

Her arm still laced through his, Evalina tightened her grip. "You've never seen him before?"

"Why such an interest in a friend of Richard's?" he responded with an impatient huff.

She looked the stranger from head to toe with obvious interest. "Let us pay our respects to Mr. Henry."

He supposed he should be assisting his sister, who had had her come-out the year before, with her marital prospects, but he had no interest at the moment.

"Perhaps later."

"You mean to look for the Baroness," she hissed in a low breath. "How am I to make a proper match if you insist upon making a fool of yourself with that woman?"

He snorted. "With your dowry, it matters little what I choose to do. Ah, I see that Aunt Louisa is returned. I leave you in her good company."

Evalina sucked in her breath. He felt her glaring into his back as he walked away, but he felt no misgiving. His sister was perfectly capable of handling herself. When they were children, she always managed to bring some castigation upon his head with their governess and their father. Even when she had instigated the mischief, he bore the brunt of the punishment. How often he had wished for a brother instead! If he had had a brother instead of a sister, the pressure upon him to marry well and produce an heir would surely not be as great. In truth, he had no great aspirations to be an earl. The responsibilities of his father were extraordinarily mundane. It was most unfair that he should limit himself simply because he was the first and only son.

At the preceding ball he had thought to quiet his father's protestations by dancing with Elisabeth Worsely, but he had not thought it would upset Abigail as much as it did. He had been careless and deserved the punishment she had bestowed upon him at Madame Botreaux's. He had to make amends. Fortunately, his father had had another flare of the gout and could not bring himself to attend the ball tonight. No doubt the old friend and banker of the family, Richard Henry, would be the eyes and ears for the Earl tonight, but Charles felt emboldened. The more his father objected, the less he attended what was said. The old man cared only for the earldom. He had no appreciation for the desires of a young man. He could not appreciate all that the Baroness offered.

Tremayne felt his body tingle with the mere thought. Tonight Lady Debarlow would be convinced of his commitment to her.

* * * * *

"If you fail to be discreet or if you disgrace the Frotham name, you will have to contend with me."

Montague looked down at the stout banker who barely stood taller than half the women in the room. If not for his wig with its prodigious front sweep, the man would not reach even the center of Montague's chest. With his rounded belly, Richard Henry reminded Montague of the Cornish game hens that the man perhaps had consumed one too many of. Many of his features tended towards the large from his bulbous nose to ears that protruded from his head like unfurled wings, save for his narrow eyes set close to one another.

"I appreciate the warning," Montague replied drily, "but you need have no fear of me. I have no cause to make public my arrangement with his lordship."

"Even so, I have arranged for an insurance on the matter."

Montague raised his brows. The glint in the little man's eyes was not promising.

"I have secured the notes upon Chelton. It cost me more than I would have wanted. Your estate apparently has some value, quite surprisingly, so that it was not so poor a business deal in the end. The notes will mature presently. If there is the slightest scandal, Chelton is forfeit to me. And I promise we shall not stop with your estate. We will claim anything of value to you. If you had children, we would arrange to possess your firstborn. We are not men to be trifled with."

His back straightening, Montague quelled the desire to drive a fist into the man's face. Perhaps he should not have accepted the Earl's offer so readily.

"We hold all the cards," Henry added with a smug grin.

"Then why make your threats to me?" Montague returned coolly. "Had you best not direct them to the Baroness?"

Henry shifted his body about as if his clothes had suddenly tightened about him. "I have spoken to the woman, but she lacks the barest sense of decency. She had the audacity to laugh in my face."

Montague smiled to himself, feeling an unexpected shred of respect for the Baroness. From what he had gathered, there was naught to commend the Baroness save her accomplishment of marrying a man of great wealth. Her present choice of lovers was, in Montague's estimation, adequate at best. Even those who considered themselves good friends of the Frotham family admitted that the Viscount was often vain and self-indulgent.

"Fortune can be a capricious nymph," Henry continued, "and has bestowed upon the Baroness far too much wealth to make any monetary inducement compelling to her. One cannot appeal to her morality for she possesses none. And our threats to have her shunned from all of polite society fall upon deaf ears. 'You cannot make me more despised than I already am' were her words. She asked if I were not aware that she was considered a jezebel and murderess? I left my meeting with her convinced that she has not all her wits about her."

Perhaps the Baroness would prove somewhat intriguing afterall, Montague considered to himself.

"Mr. Henry, how good to see you. When last you came to see my father, I had not the pleasure to greet you for you did not stay for supper."

A familiar young woman stood before them, her pale smooth skin a striking contrast to the wrinkles of her chaperone. Wearing a pink silk gown edged with white lace at the sleeves and hem, her lips colored with rouge, a blush upon her high cheekbones, she appeared a lovely flower waiting to be plucked. Estimating her age to be no more than eight and ten years of age, Montague realized where he had seen her before—in a painting hanging in the Frotham residence. She possessed the same violet eyes as the Viscount Tremayne.

"Lady Evalina, how delightful a sight you are," Henry blustered.

"Your brother must need guard you with great care for surely your loveliness will have all the young men in a row."

Frotham's daughter received the compliment with a broad smile. "You are far too kind, Mr. Henry."

She turned her sapphire eyes to Montague and waited to be introduced.

"Ah, my cousin—distant cousin," Henry provided. "Montague Edwards, may I present Lady Evalina and her aunt, Lady Louisa."

Montague bowed over Lady Evalina's hand. She allowed it to linger in his grasp until he relinquished it a second longer than might have been deemed proper. A smile hovered about her lips.

"How is it we have never met your cousin before?" she asked, her gaze still upon Montague.

"I prefer the countryside, madam," Montague supplied. He had seen the sparkle in her youthful eyes many a time before. Her interest in him was obvious, and though he found it ironic that the Earl's daughter should take an interest in him, he had no intention to veer from his assignment.

At least not yet.

"Then what brings you to town, sir?"

Montague glanced at Henry. "I could hardly refuse an invitation from Richard."

"Do you know London well, Mr. Edwards?" Lady Evalina inquired. "If not, you must have someone show you the sights. There is much to see and do here."

"I have few friends in London," Montague replied.

"Indeed? We shall have to change that, shall we not, Mr. Henry? You may be assured that any cousin of Mr. Henry is rightway a good friend of ours."

Montague smiled at the idea of being considered a friend of the Earl. He bowed. "You are generous, madam."

"A cousin?" Lady Louisa inquired as she eyed him more closely. "Which side of the family?"

"Er, my mother's side," answered Henry.

"Hm. I see no resemblance. I am sure your mother and all her family possessed fair hair."

"You might say that I am the black sheep of the family," Montague said. "I only recently discovered our relation."

Lady Louisa took no further interest in him and proceeded to detail to Henry her latest search for a balm to ease her aching joints.

"If you were to escort me to dinner," Lady Evalina said, "I could elaborate upon my favorite places. There is a menagerie at Ranalegh Gardens. I recommend it. They have an Indian tiger. Have you ever seen one? Quite frightful and ferocious beasts they are."

"Come, Evalina," Lady Louisa said, "I see that Mrs. Notting is here. I must have the name of her apothecary. She swears they make a most helpful remedy for the headache."

Lady Evalina parted with a forced smile but the air of someone confident that she would see him soon enough, a hauteur Montague was beginning to find characteristic of the Pettingtons. No doubt she had men enough wanting to be her suitors, but it was not the first time a virginal maid had shunned lads closer in age to pursue a man of greater maturity. Though a young woman's foray into the art of coquetry often amused him, he ought to disregard her advances as she was the daughter of the Earl. He would be wise to stay his distance from her, but wisdom was not a quality he always possessed in great quantity.

Before she left the room, she gave him a sidelong glance from above her fan. He decided he would escort the Lady Evalina to dinner.

* * * * *

Still no sign of the Baroness.

The society of London did not differ so greatly from that in Bath. He had even come across a number of familiar faces, all of whom were startled to find him here and even more surprised to discover he was a relation of Richard Henry. Montague could already sense the gossip about him circulating around the room, but that had never stopped women from being intrigued with him—or wanting to be in his bed.

Taking a respite from the tiresome company of Richard Henry, he searched for quiet outside upon one of the balconies overlooking the garden maze. The clouds had deserted the night sky, leaving the stars and moon to shine upon the earth below. Anticipating a moment to be alone with his thoughts, he was disappointed to find the balcony occupied.

The moonlight glanced off her gown of crimson silk and deepened the shadow between the two orbs rising beautifully above her square décolletage. She stood taller than the average woman. Montague was tall among men, and the top of her head, aided only by the heels of her silken slippers, would have grazed his nose. Her hair, unadorned, was piled high in loose curls atop her head with only four rolls gracing her nape. From her ears dangled ruby-gold earrings that lengthened the look of her neck. He found himself entranced with the area about her throat and collarbone and that swell of the bosom that separated woman from man.

She was struggling with something, a soft oath escaping lush lips. He realized she was attempting to open a snuffbox. The top, made of pearl with a scarlet phoenix painted upon it, was caught. Retrieving his own enameled box, he stepped toward her and held out the opened box.

"May I?" he offered.

She turned, startled, then glanced at his offering. Returning her own box to her reticule, she took a pinch between her thumb and forefinger and brought the snuff to her nose.

"Thank you," she said after she had inhaled the snuff. "I felt a headache come upon me."

"I had not known snuff to cure the headache," Montague remarked. "May I find you a place to sit?"

She looked him over but gave no clue as to what she thought of him. "I will stand a while longer yet. The air out here is refreshing."

He was disappointed that he could not further assist her, yet relieved that he might have a moment longer with her alone.

"That is not a trait often ascribed here in London," he said, taking a step to join her at the balcony railing.

She narrowed her eyes at him but her tone suggested she found his comment amusing.

"I only meant that I prefer it to the atmosphere inside."

"It can be rather stifling in there," he concurred. "Quite a lot of unnecessary hot air."

Again, she surveyed him with a candor that had him both unnerved and roused. She did not hide behind lowered lashes or the flutter of her fan. He wondered that she stood without a chaperone. Either she was a confirmed spinster or she was married. He glanced at the ring, a simple Gimmel band, upon her third finger, but such symbols and vows had never deterred him before.

"Indeed," she said carefully, followed by a half-smile that he found most beguiling in its irreverence.

A light breeze blew across her, and his nostrils caught a wisp of her scent. Beyond the orange blossoms in her nosegay, he detected an aroma that was hers alone. His blood pulsed bolder through his veins. He stood a hair's width closer to her than what might be deemed proper, but she did not notice or did not mind.

"Are you newly acquainted with Lord and Lady Bennington?" she asked.

"Yes. My lady is insightful."

She turned to look out over the gardens. "I am a friend of Lady Constance, Lord Bennington's sister, or I should never receive an invitation. I know the family and their friends well."

He raised his brows, but she did not elaborate.

"Perhaps you are new to London as well?"

"I had avoided it for I prefer the streets quieter and my air unsullied, but there is much to recommend the city. I am told the sights are grand. I have been advised to take myself to Ranalegh Gardens to view the Indian tiger in their menagerie. Have you seen it?"

She nodded. "A grand and majestic beast."

Her answer differed from that of Miss Evalina, and he suspected it reflected on the different nature between the two.

"You will not want for attractions or entertainment if that is what brings you to London," she added.

"At present, I am a guest of Mr. Richard Henry."

Her face darkened, and though she did not move, he sensed her withdrawal. *Damn.* He had not expected the name to displease her so and attempted to salvage his mistake. But it was too late.

"I pray you enjoy your stay in London, sir," she said and turned upon her heel.

Montague could only study the curve of her back as she walked back inside. Considering his current commission, his interest in this woman was ill advised, yet he very much wanted another opportunity with the woman on the balcony. He hoped that seducing the Baroness would not prove a lengthy endeavor. When he was done with the Baroness, he would seek this mysterious woman and make her his.

* * * * *

"That man were devilishly handsome," said Lady Constance, her emerald eyes sparkling. "He is more rugged than your young Viscount."

Abigail glanced back in the direction of the balcony where she had stood but said nothing. She would admit that she had found the stranger attractive, but that was before he had revealed himself a friend of Richard Henry.

Lady Constance poked her in the arm with her fan. "And how wicked of him to corner you out there in the dark."

"There was light enough from the moon and stars," Abigail replied.

"A romantic setting indeed."

Abigail shook her head at her friend of many years. The two stood in an anteroom as they waited for the dinner announcement. Lady Constance had been one of few willing to befriend Abigail before she had become the Baroness Debarlow.

"He offered me his snuffbox and nothing more."

Lady Constance drew her bright red lips down into a mock pout. "Because you did not provide him enough time."

"He is a guest of that odious Mr. Henry."

"Admittedly, that is a mark against his favor, but the gentleman is no less pleasing to the eye. I should have no hesitation to find myself situated in his arms—or his bed."

"A handsome form does not distinguish him as a good lover. Charles is one such illustration that a beautiful countenance does not beget abilities of that nature."

With some direction, he could prove himself, at best, adequate to the task, Abigail thought to herself, recollecting how Charles was quick to throw up her skirts after a few simple kisses upon her neck and breast. The Viscount had in him too much conceit clouding his ability to learn and hence excel.

"It is manifest in his manners and in the way he *moves,*" Constance insisted.

Abigail thought back to the moment on the balcony. Certainly the stranger exuded a sensual confidence both quiet and understated, unlike the cocky swagger of Charles. The stranger had stood just close enough for her to sense the warmth of his body in the evening air, and she would not deny to Constance that she did not feel herself stirred by his presence. But even had he not admitted to being a friend of Richard Henry, she would not be distracted from her efforts with the Viscount. If she had liberty to pursue another man, it would be the Marquess of Dunnesford.

"I think I should introduce myself to this man," Constance continued, "save that he seems to only have eyes for you."

Abigail looked around and found the stranger across the room staring at her. Beside him stood that corpulent, overindulgent Richard Henry. She resisted the instinct to raise an indignant brow and merely looked away to Constance.

"No doubt he will want nothing of me after hearing what Mr. Henry has to say in my favor," Abigail responded.

"He does not appear to be disturbed."

"My dear, you do not need my permission to pursue him."

"Of course. It does not dissuade me even were he to take an

interest in you. He is far too appealing an item not to sample."

"I wish you much success."

"And you? I have yet to set eyes on the Viscount tonight."

"He is tasked with showing me his devotion tonight. I shall allow him to make love to me—"

"Here?"

"I would value a recommendation."

"The East Library. No one will be there. Even my brother fails to enter that room."

"The East Library then."

"While you woo Tremayne, I shall apply myself to our new guest."

Abbey avoided looking in the direction of the stranger for she had no wish to have him misconstrue a glance, Abigail prepared to enter the dining hall, but she could not shake the sense that his gaze was still upon her, and that made her breath uneven.

* * * * *

Montague could hardly believe the woman of the balcony and the Baroness Debarlow were one in the same. Whether it be Fortune or the Strangeness of Fate remained to be seen, but he could not help but be even more intrigued by the woman. From where he sat at the long baronial dinner table, he had a fair view of the Baroness sitting opposite him but eight chairs removed. He had seen her cursory glance in the anteroom, and it was clear to him that she, unlike her friend, had no interest in furthering an acquaintance with him.

She did not strike him as the sort of woman to be drawn to the likes of Viscount Tremayne. She conveyed far too much maturity and intelligence. From what he had observed, she seemed to pay no attention to the Viscount, barely glancing in his direction throughout dinner. He wondered as to the nature of their relationship and looked over to Lady Constance. From their easy manner with each other, he discerned them to be good friends. Perhaps the Lady Constance could shed some light onto the matter.

As he spooned his soup, he saw from the corner of his eye the Baroness having a word with one of the serving the next course, a roast pudding. She slipped him a note. The servant glanced in the direction of the Viscount, who sat at the far end of the table with his sister and their aunt, and nodded. The server slipped the note into the cuff of his coat. Montague finished off his soup and waited for the servant, who would have to finish serving the rest of the table before he could have the opportunity to make his way to the end where the Viscount sat.

"A crown for the *billet doux* you hold," Montague said in a low voice to the servant as he was being served.

"Sir?"

"The one in the cuff of your coat sleeve."

The young server paused but lowered his arm beneath the table. Montague retrieved the slip of paper and replaced it with a crown. Opening the note, he saw only a few words.

East Library.
Eleven o' clock.

Folding the note, Montague tucked it into his coat pocket. Lady Fortune had provided him the opportunity to resume his encounter with the Baroness Debarlow.

CHAPTER FOUR

RECLINING ON A SETTEE in the darkness of the library, Abigail pressed her fingers into her temple as she closed her eyes. Her headache had returned, but she would not have it deter her plans with Charles. She intended a special treat this night. One that would leave him longing for more and compel him to weigh the bounty that awaited him should he secure her in marriage. They would wed in Gretna Green, furthering the scandal of their matrimony. And she would at last have her revenge upon the Earl of Frotham.

A minuet played faintly from behind closed doors. The clouds that had been absent hours ago when she had stood upon the balcony with the stranger had emerged and flitted across the moon, leaving scant light to illuminate the room. She recalled the stranger. Constance spoke true—the man was handsome, but it was not merely a pleasing countenance that Abigail felt drawn to. Accustomed to the smiles of men trying to charm themselves into her bed, she found the serious set of the stranger's jaw to be…interesting. She also felt drawn to the depth of his eyes. Though she might ascribe their mystery to the darkness of night, she believed that they were wont to reveal little. She could usually discern a man's interest in her within moments of their first encounter, but the thoughts of this one were harder to determine. After she was married to Charles, she might consider pursuing a man such as the stranger. It was a shame that he was a friend of Richard Henry or she would have contested Constance for the man's attention. Despite her flippant remarks about being in a man's bed, Lady Constance had little desire to dismay her beloved brother.

EM BROWN

The grandfather clock in the corner of the room chimed the eleventh hour, and she heard the door of the library open. When first they had met, Charles was not wont to be prompt, but she had trained him well since then that tardiness had its consequences.

"Close the door behind you," she instructed.

He did as told and the room fell once more into darkness.

"My feet are weary from standing. You may tend to them."

She kicked off her slippers and draped her ankles over the arm of the settee. There was a pause, and just before she was about to admonish him for not scurrying to her bidding, she heard him move towards the end of the settee. He lifted her right foot in a firm but gentle hold, then ran a knuckle up along her instep. The sensation surprised her. She had expected Charles to begin rubbing recklessly. She had not expected him capable of a finer touch. Perhaps she should have provided him more opportunity ere now.

He slid his knuckle back down, and she inadvertently shivered despite her intention to remain stoic. It would not do to allow Charles to think that he had any undue influence upon her or her body. Slowly, and with the perfect amount of pressure, he stroked the bottom of her foot. She could feel herself relaxing into the rhythmic stroking. He pressed both thumbs where the backside of his finger had been and began rubbing the arch of her foot. She suppressed a satisfied moan. She had commanded him to tend to her feet thinking that they were symbols of his further submission, not realizing they could feel so sensuous. As he caressed her entire foot, with attention to every toe, she felt her headache lighten. Clearly, Charles had been taking lessons from someone. For once, she was impressed.

"And what else are you capable of?" she murmured when he had finished with her other foot.

She heard him walk around the back of the settee. When she felt a hand at her collar, she stirred at his nearness to her neck. He allowed his hand to rest upon her without moving until she relaxed back into the pillow. He took the hand that covered her eyes and laid it gently beside her body. With both hands he massaged her shoulders, pressing his fingers and thumbs into her flesh with gentle but increasing pressure. His hands felt warm and strong upon her. Gad but if she had known Charles capable of such pleasurable touch, she would have commanded him to tend to her more often!

When he began to caress her neck, her body melted. With one hand he cupped the nape of her neck and kneaded away the last of her tensions. He stretched her neck and threaded his fingers through her hair to massage her scalp. Taking in a deep breath, she was conscious of the air moving through her nostrils, invigorating her senses. To her surprise, she even felt desire stirring. He had finally acquired the touch of a lover, finding parts of her that she had never before considered caressing but that now wanted for more attention.

"You have done well," she remarked when he had finished. "I am quite pleased."

"Your servant, my lady."

Her eyes flew open. The voice was familiar but it did not belong to Charles!

"Who—" she began to demand.

Suddenly the room was flooded with light as Lady Constance opened the door.

"Abbey, I thought you should know that the Viscount—oh!"

Abigail sat up and looked over the settee at her friend, who had halted nonplussed at the threshold, and that of the stranger, who stood calmly near her beside the settee.

"Pardon the intrusion!" Constance said, a mischievous smile tugging at the corner of her lips, before leaving the room, closing the door behind her.

Abigail and the stranger were thrown back into darkness.

"I think some light is in order," she said with more calm than she felt.

The man obliged, finding a tinderbox at a table near the settee and lighting the lamp. Sitting up, she eyed him carefully. He submitted himself to her scrutiny without word.

"Who are you?" she asked.

4

"Montague Edwards," he replied with a bow.

"Why were you attempting to impersonate the Viscount Tremayne?"

"It was not my intention to impersonate anyone."

"Then why were you—why did you do what you did?"

He did not flinch and answered as if she were merely inquiring into the weather. "I walked into the room, and a woman bade me tend to her weary feet. I think it would have been ungentlemanly not to accommodate her request."

She flushed, realizing it was true that she had simply assumed the man to have been Charles. Nonetheless, this Mr. Edwards was an uncommon man to have obeyed her directive without question. But perhaps it was just as preposterous to think that he was attempting to impersonate someone?

As if reading her mind, he said, "I had thought to find solitude and, in truth, respite. I was wearied by the company I keep."

She raised her eyebrows, wondering if he was referring to Richard Henry. If so, he was a little elevated in her estimation.

"But I am clearly not the individual you were hoping for and will take my leave."

He stared at her, as if to say "lest my lady requires more tending to," before bowing and departing. He had very penetrating eyes, she observed. Her heart beat a little more rapidly. The thought of his touch upon her once more made her shiver, and she very much wanted to stay his presence, but she allowed him to leave. Surely she had imagined that his eyes spoke to her. Or was he as brazen as he was uncommon?

She settled back into the settee, unsure of herself and unsettled that she should feel such doubt. Montague Edwards was not part of her plans, and she should pay him no further heed. But it was no easy matter to forget how his hands had made her feel. How glorious it would be to receive such treatment each and every day! Even now, her body responded with a memory all its own. She closed her eyes and replayed his massage upon her. She repeated his name in her mind, wondering if she had ever heard of him before.

It was not until later when she had finally composed herself and left the library that she had forgotten to ask herself what had become of the Viscount.

* * * * *

Montague had not wanted to leave the library, but he could not appear too eager whilst she was still aloof. She did not trust men readily. He could sense, despite her stoic physiognomy, that he had rattled her. He had stated the truth that it had not been his intention to impersonate the Viscount for he had not expected to walk into a dark room and be commanded to do anything. He had intended to feign surprise to find anyone in the room, explain that he had expected to seek and obtain solitude, and hopefully strike up a more satisfactory conversation with her. She had presented the opportunity, the invitation—nay, the demand—to touch her. And he could not resist.

There was no mistaking the stirring in his groin as his hands roamed over her supple skin. He was pleased to feel such desire for it would fuel his efforts. He had feared that a seduction born of necessity rather than aspiration would lack the passion needed for success. He wanted to bed the Baroness and not merely for the sake of his arrangement with the Earl. She had expressed her pleasure with his caresses—even had she not put words to her sentiments, he could detect it from the responses of her body—and he wanted to show her how much more awaited her enjoyment. What words or sounds of satisfaction would she utter when he had her writhing beneath him?

Returning to the ballroom, he straightened his shoulders and looked about the room for Lady Constance. She could aid his endeavor if he could win her over. He had learned from Mr. Henry that the she and the Baroness were indeed bosom friends, and that were it not for the good graces of Lady Constance, the Baroness might have been shunned altogether from polite society. With women, it was often necessary to court the friend as well. Woe to the man who incurred the rancor of a woman's best friend.

He found the Lady Constance cornered at one end of the ballroom by a woman wearing a headdress with exceptionally high ostrich plumes.

From the downturn in her lips, he perceived that the Lady Constance was not enamored of the other woman.

"Tremayne has not asked my Elisabeth for a single dance!" the feathered woman said.

"It would appear the Viscount has not asked any woman to dance," Lady Constance replied evenly and made a move to indicate her intention to leave, but Mrs. Worsely did not budge.

"Because he waits for the Baroness Debarlow! I tell you that I shall not tolerate such humiliation. My Elisabeth is worth twenty of her."

"Miss Worsely will not want for suitors. Perhaps—"

"You could do polite society a grand favor by convincing that woman to release Tremayne from her claws."

"You mistake the amount of influence I—"

"Have you tried to reason with her? Has she not the least sense of propriety? Her conduct is most inappropriate, even for her standards. You must advise her to cease. If I may, you have a responsibility, Lady Constance, aye, a duty to—"

Montague decided to interject. "Lady Constance, I have been looking all over for you."

Both women turned to look at him in surprise.

"Did you not promise me this minuet?" he finished as he offered his arm.

"Er—yes," Lady Constance replied, hastily taking his arm without a glance back at Mrs. Worsely.

He led her onto the dance floor.

"My knight in shining armor," she whispered to him as they took their positions to the start of the music.

She had an engaging, if crooked, smile, Montague thought to himself as he bowed to her curtsy. He turned his side to hers and took her elevated hand. They stepped forward together.

"I hope you will forgive my earlier intrusion," she said to him.

"There is naught to forgive, my lady," Montague responded. "It was fortunate that you came upon us when you did. I believe I was mistaken for another and not the gentleman your friend expected."

"Ah, yes."

"Please convey to her my regrets for having spoiled her

rendezvous. I realize I had departed without apologizing."

"Forgive me, but you do not sound remorseful, sir."

His eyebrows rose at her impudence, but he suppressed a smile. "What do you imply, my lady?"

As she finished walking around him and resumed her spot, she replied in a low voice, "I have not known any man to regret his time with Lady Debarlow."

"My lady is most astute. I confess that I felt our time in the library short-lived, but I did not mean to cause distress."

"She is a woman of confidence. Are you quite sure she was distressed?"

Montague thought back to the library. Save for her initial disbelief at finding herself with another man instead of the Viscount, the Baroness had every appearance of composure.

"Perhaps it was a pleasant surprise," Lady Constance added after completing a bouree.

"I should be relieved if that were the case, but I fear I shall never know. I could not help but overhear Mrs. Worsely. It appears that Lady Debarlow is spoken for."

He could see the wheels of her mind turning as she curtsied to the woman opposite him. When the women had completed their steps, he took his turn.

"Have you been to Berkshire" she asked after he had returned to his position beside her.

"Not in many years."

Her eyes twinkled. "My brother has a small estate there. I have asked Abbey to join me there. Perhaps you could call upon us when we are there?"

Montague paused. "To what do I owe such generosity?"

She briefly frowned, but the mischievous half-smile returned soon enough. "Let us say that I believe my dear friend is in need of better *divertissement*."

"You flatter me."

"Do not fail me, Mr. Edwards."

Montague smiled. "Perish the thought."

CHAPTER FIVE

"THE CAVERN OF PLEASURES?" Montague repeated as he took his breakfast in bed the following morning.

Jonathan grinned. "A den of debauchery for the Quality. The proprietress is one Penelope Botreaux."

"And you followed the Baroness into this place?" Montague asked as he handed Jonathan a cup of coffee.

Downing the beverage in two gulps, Jonathan sat down in a chair across from the bed. When in private, Montague allowed the valet a degree of latitude. The two had been in far too many scrapes together to adhere to the formalities between servant and master.

"She went in, but I did not. When the door opened briefly, I saw a sentry of sorts inside. I worried that the Baroness would discover me if I were to follow her in."

Montague nodded. "But how do you know the place then?"

"I stood about across the street, and within the half hour a coach pulled up to the gate. A man debarked and went inside, but his coachman tarried outside. I had with me a bottle of gin—if ever the Baroness found and confronted me, I would play a disorderly drunkard—and walked by the man. 'Your master has you employed a late hour, my good fellow,' I say to him. 'Aye,' he grumbles. I offer him a swig from my bottle and say, 'Mine is afeared to walk the streets alone, but he was determined to come here. What is this place?' The man snorts, 'First time, eh?' That is when he tells me what he knows, which, in truth, be not much for he has only ever had to wait outside the gates. What he knows he has gleaned from others like him. I ask of him how he knows what he has heard to be true. His master, he tells me, always returns with a funny gait. And ever since the man has become a patron of Madame Botreaux, he has not once returned to the banios of Covent Garden where he used to frequent."

"Does he know the other patrons?"

"He mentioned a few names, all unfamiliar to me. He said there is much secrecy to the place and that most take great care to conceal their identities."

Montague allowed his toast to grow cool for he was in too much thought. What would bring the Lady Debarlow to such a place?

"The Baroness strode to the door without hesitation," Jonathan offered, "as if she had been there before. She must have stayed an hour or so. When she emerged, she had upon her a cloak and got into a chair. I followed her to her residence and saw no more of her."

Was the Baroness entertaining another lover? Montague wondered. He was convinced the Viscount was no match for Lady Debarlow. But the existence of another paramour would complicate his plans. But why would the Lady Constance reference the need for a better diversion if the Baroness had another? Was the Lady Constance unaware of a second lover or did she disapprove of both men?

"I must find a way into this Cavern," Montague thought aloud as he tossed aside the bedcovers and rose from bed.

"For the Baroness or your own purpose?" Jonathan asked, rising to his feet to finish what remained of Montague's breakfast.

"It would depend, eh, on the exact nature of the establishment?"

Jonathan finished off the toast in two mouthfuls. "I think the name tells it all."

Montague shed his nightshirt and went to the water basin to wash his face. The Baroness was proving more and more intriguing. Sleep had eluded him last night as he reflected upon the events of the night. The scent of her, the sounds, and the feel of her body beneath his hands. All continued to barrage his memory. The moon had emerged from the clouds just prior to the interruption by Lady Constance, allowing him to study the pout of her lips, the point of her nose, the curve of her ear.

Only her hand over her eyes prevented him for beholding all of her face.

He had enjoyed her responses to his touch and found himself wanting to elicit more from her. He had skimmed his fingers beneath the back collar of her gown. He would have liked to massage her bare shoulders or caress the flat below her collarbone, just above the tops of her breasts. But he was satisfied that he had left her with just enough of a taste to tease her appetite.

"Have my card sent to Madame Botreaux," Montague instructed. "I should very much like to meet this proprietress of the *Cavern of Pleasures*."

* * * * *

Penelope Botreaux enjoyed reclining on the settee in the pose of a lazy Dionysus. From her Rubenesque figure, Montague surmised her to have also enjoyed her share of fine wines and foods. Her dress of delicate muslin draped over thin layers of petticoats harkened to ancient Grecian attire. Sandaled feet revealing painted toes peeked from underneath her gown. She peered at him from behind her quizzing glass, boldly raking her gaze across his body, perhaps envisioning how he would appear before her sans any clothing. The proprietress had responded swiftly, inviting him to call upon her within days of receiving his card.

Montague calmly submitted himself to her scrutiny in the dim drawing room. Nothing in the nicely appointed but unpretentious address gave any evidence that another world lay within. A handsome young man stood behind her holding a tray with two glasses of wine. Thinking back to the striking footman who had answered the door, Montague idly wondered if all her servants were such sweets for the eye.

"Pray have a glass of sherry with me." Madame Botreaux gestured to her servant.

Montague accepted the offering.

"Now, Mr. Edwards, what is the purpose of your call?" she asked, taking a sip of the dark liquid between two vibrantly rouged lips.

"I am interested in your *establishment*," he replied.

"Indeed?"

"I understand it to be quite exceptional in nature."

"Yes, but its success depends in part on its exclusivity. Not anyone can become a member lest they have been referred by a patron in good standing."

"I see. I fear I know not your patrons and, thus, cannot secure such a reference," he said candidly. "Might there be another means to recommend my application?"

She looked him over once more with studied interest. She ran her tongue over her lower lip, either in response to the taste of the wine or what she saw. He wondered if she might require him to strip naked as part of his application.

"I understand you to have had a repute of sorts in Bath."

"My lady has inquired about me," he noted. "May I ask if she found the information to her liking?"

She smiled. "It does not displease me. In truth, I am intrigued that you have not been expelled from polite society there given your exploits."

"May I be bold but candid?" he asked, though he knew the answer. It was obvious there was no need to be timid with Madame Botreaux.

"You may."

"I do not consider my liaisons to be exploits. Unlike the common rakehell who uses and discards women like so many handkerchiefs, I exalt the female sex."

"You have left a trail of broken hearts, no?"

"But not without hope."

She thought for a moment. "Dues for the year are paid in advance. I also recommend generous perquisites for those attending the members. Unhappy servants can be quite loquacious."

"I understand."

"Would you care to view the facility before you make your decision? Some of our activities are not for the faint of heart."

"Your hospitality is appreciated, my lady. May I?"

Standing up, he proffered his arm. She placed her wine glass back on the tray of her manservant and took his arm.

"Lovely," she murmured, feeling the muscle beneath her hand.

"Tell me, does the proprietress take part in the activities of the *Cavern?*"

"I do not intermingle with the membership if that is your query, save for a select few that are in my confidence. But that does not prevent me from *appreciating* my members."

She guided him down the hallway. Pointing to a series of doors on either side, she said, "Patrons may use these rooms for their toilette. A valet or chambermaid is always available to assist."

Pulling him over to one of the rooms, she opened the door to a room that was perhaps once a small library. A single bookcase remained but instead of books, it held a series of masks, ranging from the austere to ornate. She selected a simple black mask that covered three quarters of the face, leaving only the mouth and chin visible.

"I think you will look quite nice in this one," she told him and slipped it over his face.

For herself she selected an ivory mask trimmed with pearls and feathers. She led him back outside. At the end of the hall, they reached a simple door that looked as if it might have led to the kitchen. He opened the door to a winding staircase. If not for the sconces upon the walls, they would have entered complete darkness. The first sound to greet his ears was a woman's high pitched scream. If not for the knowledge of where he was, he might have thought the woman to be in peril.

"Ah, the sweet sounds of tormented pleasure," Madame Botreaux observed, eying Montague for his reaction.

He did not flinch, but his blood began to course more strongly as they rounded the corner and came into view of the assembly hall. The vision was unlike any he had ever seen. The assembly hall had the appearance of a half-finished structure that had sunk into the ground. The walls of the alcoves lining the main assembly area were of rock, but the floor of the assembly itself was of perfectly smooth marble. A single chandelier above the assembly floor, strategically placed candelabras and fireplaces provided just enough light and warmth.

Men and women in various states of dress occupied both the main assembly and the alcoves. While some were clothed from neck to foot, others were stripped to the buff. Montague observed one woman wearing naught but nettle branches wrapped about her loins. In one corner a man wore only a lady's corset and petticoats. His partner had not a shred of clothing, proudly baring his assets for all to behold. A woman dressed in the costume of an Amazonian warrior led a man wearing only a loincloth about the assembly floor by a chain around his neck. He crawled after her upon all fours and, like a dog, licked at her heels.

In one of the alcoves, Montague witnessed a woman, her beautiful slender body suspended from the ceiling, being whipped alternately by a man and woman. In the neighboring alcove, a man had pinned a woman against the wall with her legs wrapped about his hips. She clawed at his back while he thrust into her. Beside the pair, a man lay with two women upon a mattress, their naked forms silhouetted by the fireplace behind them. As he kissed and fondled the breasts of one woman, the other had taken his cock full into her mouth.

The sinners of the second level of Dante's Inferno could not have engaged in more carnal decadence.

"Do you like what you see?" Madame Botreaux asked.

"Undoubtedly," Montague replied, his cock stirring at the lustful images before him. "You have quite the establishment, my lady. How did you come to oversee such an enterprise?"

"Years ago, my husband and I—ah, you are surprised that I was married?"

"Only in that I would not have expected a woman such as yourself to have confined herself to matrimony."

"Marriage itself places no constraints. Only man."

Montague considered the possible truth of her words. He had never considered matrimony anything but constraining.

"You are fortunate to have found a man of similar pursuits, one free of mind."

"You speak as if such a person were a rarity. Though my husband and I enjoyed the company of others, we loved one another above all. I would not have wished myself married to any other. He passed away before his due, and there is not a day that goes by in which I do not miss him."

Taken aback by this revelation, Montague had no response. He had thought himself broad of mind, unhindered by prim convention or orthodoxy, but he had not considered that sentimentality could be coupled with lust.

"Such love must be a precious and blessed gift."

"Aye, but you do not appear to me, sir, as one who places much stock in Providence."

It was his turn to study her. "My lady?"

"You would say that you are a man who makes his own destiny?"

"Without doubt."

"Love is not something that falls from the sky. It is there for the taking."

This was an odd turn in their *tete-a-tete*, but he felt comfortable enough in her presence to speak his mind.

"Love has not been a pursuit of mine. A man has other concerns to occupy his mind."

"You think love be reserved only for the puerile romantic or the weaker sex?"

"I mean only to convey that it has not been a priority of mine."

"What a pity."

Her response startled him. Was she not the proprietress of debauchery, the provider of indulgence and wantoness?

They descended the stairs down to the assembly floor.

"My husband discovered this building," she went on. "We would meet with another couple of like mind every week and easily found more who shared our 'spirit of adventure.' We wanted a place to indulge our desires away from prying eyes."

"You have sustained quite the institution."

"I take great pride in what I do. Tell me, are you of a certain persuasion? I can assist you in finding your place."

He scanned the entire assembly to see what drew his interest most. His gaze settled upon a woman wearing a black corset, layers of black petticoats, and black lace gloves. Her burgundy mask, shaped like a butterfly and edged with black lace, covered most of her face, including her cheeks, but left open the area from nose to chin. Her chin, with its slight protrusion noticeable only in profile, was familiar to him. She stood in one of the alcoves, a riding crop tucked in her underarm, and retrieved from her pockets a snuffbox. She attempted to open it, but the lid would not oblige. Resigning, she returned the box to its place amidst her petticoats. Montague would have wagered the box to be made of pearl with a scarlet phoenix upon its cover.

"What persuasion is she?" he asked with little attempt at nonchalance.

Madame Botreaux followed his stare. "At present she is a Mistress, but that is not her true persuasion. In all her years here when she came with her hus…she prefers to play the submissive."

"She is a longtime member of yours?"

Madame Botreaux eschewed the question by asking, "You have an interest in her?"

He considered taking the proprietress into his confidence and decided there was no harm in acknowledging her observation. "I should like to make her acquaintance."

"At present she seems to have dedicated herself to one submissive. If you wish to take his place or join him, you must first offer yourself up first at the Presenting. It is a little custom we have for new members."

"And if I wish to play the dominant role?"

"The submissives present themselves first for the veteran members to select from. Then the dominants present themselves. Veteran members may offer themselves first for selection."

He wanted to know whom the Baroness had chosen as her submissive and decided to stall for time.

"Are there rules that I should be aware of?"

"How familiar are you to the ways of the dominant?"

Montague thought back to his many different lovers. He had on one occasion spanked a woman, but nothing he had done was on the order of what was practiced at the *Cavern*.

"My experience is limited," he admitted, "but I am a quick study."

Especially with the right woman, he thought to himself as he kept his eye on the Baroness. At that moment, a masked man with dark hair ran into the alcove and promptly kneeled before her. He wore only breeches. But from his height and size, Montague suspected the man might be the Viscount Tremayne. He felt a twinge of jealousy. Why was the Baroness squandering her time with Tremayne? Surely among the many patrons of the *Cavern* she could another willing to take his place.

"And I could be a good mentor."

Montague looked down at Madame Botreaux. She was older and a little more corpulent than any lover he had been with but not entirely unattractive if she did not paint herself with quite so much rouge, which lent her the appearance of an aged cherub with her rounded face.

"Dare I merit such an honor?" he returned before glancing back in the direction of the Baroness.

He watched the Viscount kissing the laces of her boots before rising to his feet. Lady Debarlow said something to Tremayne, who proceeded to shed his breeches without hesitation. Without doubt she could do better, he considered as he assessed the unimpressive size of the cock jutting from the Viscount. He returned his attention to the Baroness. Her provocative ensemble displayed her bare shoulders, as lovely as he suspected they would be would from what he had seen at the Bennington ball. Her petticoats reached to the middle of her shins, leaving a glimpse of her legs above her ankle-length boots. The Baroness lashed her crop against Tremayne's buttocks. He winced but his erection grew harder. Montague found himself equally aroused.

"You are agreeable to me," Madame Botreaux said.

Lady Debarlow placed her hand about the Viscount's erection and rubbed the shaft. Montague wondered at the sensation of lace against skin there. The Viscount appeared to moan. The Baroness stepped away and landed three more blows against his arse. Then ground her hand once more against his cock.

"I thought the proprietress did not engage with her patrons?" Montague inquired. Had Jonathan tied his cravat tighter than usual today?

As Madame Botreaux considered his question, he watched the Baroness alternate between lashing at the Viscount and fondling his cock. At one point, she stood with her bosom against his chest and licked his earlobe. The sight of her pink tongue darting from between her lips had Montague cursing the sweltering mask he wore. He needed a breath of cool air.

"I can always make an exception," Madame Botreaux replied.

Montague smiled at her. To gain admittance—and access to the Baroness—he would consider laying with the plump and shameless proprietress.

At that moment the Viscount roared as the ministrations of the Baroness brought him to climax. The seed shot from his cock as his body convulsed. The Baroness whipped him a few more times. He fell to his knees.

"Perhaps we must need begin your lessons at present?" Madame Botreaux said with a pointed glance at the bulge in his breeches.

Montague said nothing but he felt he could fuck a hole in the wall if it would relieve the pressure he felt. There was no question that he would have to make the Baroness his. And not because of his agreement with the Earl. He wanted her attentions upon his body. He wanted her naked and writhing against him. He wanted her more than he could remember wanting any other woman. The thought unnerved him.

CHAPTER SIX

A FORTNIGHT HAD passed since the Bennington ball and still Abigail could not rid her thoughts of Montague Edwards even as she rode her mare at full gallop through the fields of Lord Bennington's estate in Berkshire. Perhaps in her quest to conquer the affections of Charles she had forgotten what it felt like to be touched by a man such as Montague. Or perhaps her menses were upon her, making her acutely aware of the desires of her body. She had fondled herself a number of times in memory of what had transpired in that library, but the resulting satisfaction did not diminish the deeper longing.

She slowed her mare upon reaching the top of a small hill. The wind had blown her coiffure loose and tipped her bonnet awry, but the run had reminded her there were other ways to thrill her body. She had relished the wind pressing against her face and streaming through her hair. The pumping of horse flesh beneath her, the rhythmic pounding of the hoofs made the blood course vibrantly through her body.

Taking in several breaths of air, she contemplated the hills before her.

"Are you preparing to make a run at Ascot?" Constance asked, trotting her horse up to Abigail.

The open hills beckoned, but a light mist had begun descending from the clouds and Abigail knew that Constance would wish to head back before nightfall. The rose of dusk had begun blooming across the grey skies.

"Methinks that someone may be in need of a decent tumble in the sack to calm her nerves?"

Abigail glanced at her friend, whose bonnet sat perfectly in place atop her dark brown curls. "And people think *me* the scandalous one."

The two women turned their horses around and rode back at a leisurely place.

"A good tumble can be as sublime as a glass of wine, and in truth, I think I should always prefer the former to the latter."

Abigail shook her head. "My dear, have you no other thoughts?"

"You do not fool me, Baroness. Your *eros* is as strong as mine. The Viscount cannot satisfy you even if you afforded the pup an opportunity."

"He may yet surprise me."

Constance snorted. "If you believed that, why have you not invited him into your bed ere now?"

"I had every intention—at your brother's ball. My plans were disrupted."

"By a true man. Do you not yearn for the touch of a man?"

Abigail thought of Montague Edwards and then of the Marquess of Dunnesford. The mere thought of these two men made her body tingle with warmth.

"I have not taken myself to a nunnery," she responded. "I simply have no wish to disrupt my efforts with Charles. If he should become jealous and withdraw, all my pains would be for naught."

"He need not know…" Constance pressed.

"If I promise to fuck a man when I am done with Charles, will you consider the matter at rest?"

"I merely have your well-being in mind. Admittedly, I have not your fortitude. I cannot conceive of being with the Viscount in any manner given what he had done. I should think that *not* lifting your skirts to him would be more of a punishment."

"Aye, but such deprivation does not leave a lasting mark with men. I have only to recall the situation of poor Libby to reinforce my patience. But I have not the fortitude you think or I should still sleep in my old bedchamber."

Libby was a young maid who had come upon the Debarlow house seeking employment. Though heavy with child, she had managed to disguise her small abdomen from all but the most discerning eye. The Debarlow housekeeper had turned her out for she came with no references, and Abigail had discovered the young woman upon the steps weeping.

With dark circles beneath her eyes, hollow cheeks, and pale countenance, Libby had appeared quite sickly. Abigail had invited the maidservant into the house and offered her tea and bread. Libby nearly swallowed the bread whole and, upon finishing, begged for more. Abigail had more bread brought with ham and meatpie, all of which Libby finished as if she had not eaten in days, and perhaps she had not. Once she had eaten her fill, she thanked Abigail and promptly burst into tears.

"My dear, pray do not trouble yourself," Abigail had said. "I shall have Cook wrap some ham and cheese for you to take when you leave."

Her words made Libby cry harder. "You are Kindness itself, m'lady."

Abigail gave Libby a handkerchief from her reticule and brushed away a tendril of the maid's ebony hair. Despite her red swollen eyes, Libby was a lovely creature.

"I am lost!" Libby sobbed into the handkerchief. "Surely there is not a more wretched being than I!"

"Come, it cannot be as dismal as you say."

Libby shook her head and hid her face in the handkerchief.

Abigail took a seat by the young woman on the settee. Her appointment with the seamstress in Mayfair would have to wait.

"I will not render judgment, so you may speak plain," she said. "But what has caused such grief for you?"

Libby hesitated. She glanced at Abigail before hanging her head and replying, "I h-have been seeking—seeking employment for a fortnight. I-I've no place to—to…"

The cries overcame her.

Abigail tried a simpler question. "Where were you employed

previously and in what capacity?"

"As a m-maidservant for the Earl of Frotham."

Abigail felt her back stiffen. "And what prompted your departure?"

Again, Libby shook her head and saturated the handkerchief with her tears. "I am too—too ashamed to speak of it, m'lady. Only—only I am forsaken!"

"I cannot promise that I can be of assistance, but you've naught to fear from me no matter how grave the truth."

When the sobs had turned into sniffles, Libby ventured to tell a little of her story. She had fallen for the young and handsome Viscount Tremayne. His attentions had overwhelmed her and she thought herself to be in love. She had lain with him and was now with child. When she had revealed her state to him, he became a different person: the warm, gay demeanor replaced with cold aloofness. He recommended she see a doctor who could put an end to her condition. It was evident he wanted nothing more to do with her. When the housekeeper discovered the state of affairs—the woman had harbored suspicions for some time— she dismissed the maid.

Upon hearing that Libby had no family, Abigail had decided to find a post for the maid within the Debarlow household. Three months later Libby gave birth to a boy who had every appearance of being a Frotham despite its infancy. Some weeks after the birth, Libby had, against the advice of Abigail, sought out Charles to recognize his son. Abigail knew not what had transpired, but Libby had returned home sobbing. Later that night, Abigail had discovered the maid swinging from the chandelier of her bedchamber. After two sleepless nights in which she would sit in her bed and stare at the chandelier, Abigail decided to move into one of the smaller bedchambers down the hall. On occasion, she thought she could still hear the echoes of Libby sobbing.

Abigail had been able to locate Libby's grandmother, who lived in a small village near Wales. The woman was grieved to hear of Libby's fate and had agreed to care for the baby boy. As the woman was of modest means, Abigail had promised to provide funds to help care for the boy until he reached maturity.

Libby had named her son Charles.

* * * * *

As she removed her riding gloves and entered the charming country house of Lord Bennington, Abigail determined that for the next few days she should put aside all thoughts of Charles, or any other man for that matter, and enjoy the races and the scenery. But her resolution was shortlived for in the drawing room stood two gentlemen. One she did not recognize immediately. The other was Montague Edwards.

"Mr. Holmes, Mr. Edwards," Constance greeted. "What a pleasant surprise. My brother is still out hunting roe. He would be at it *ad infinitum* if the sun did not set. I pray you will make yourselves comfortable."

Abigail looked at her friend with suspicion. Was the presence of these two men indeed a 'surprise?' She now recognized Latimer Holmes, but she did not think either of the two were well acquainted with the Benningtons. The two men bowed to Constance and then to her in turn. It seemed to her that Montague's gaze lingered upon her longer. She felt a flurry up her spine.

"I think you know the Baroness Debarlow?"

"Your servant, my lady," Latimer bowed after removing his hat.

Edwards repeated the genuflection, but the intensity of his stare instantly brought to mind the intimacy they had shared.

"Pray take a seat, and I shall have tea brought in," gestured Constance cheerfully as she rang for the tea.

The two men sat down upon the sofa. Leaning back, Edwards crossed one leg over the other, displaying a chiseled leg. He was no less dapper in his traveling clothes.

Abigail chose to sit in a chair facing away from the window and setting sun.

"Your brother is most generous to have extended us an invitation to stay," Latimer remarked.

Abigail glanced sharply at Constance, who had refused to look in her direction thus far. She found it hard to believe that her friend would not have known about the guests.

"Do you know Lord Bennington well then?" Abigail asked.

"You know my brother's fondness for the hunt," Constance replied. "Mr. Holmes is quite the experienced hunter."

"Indeed? And is your preferred prey of choice the same as Lord Bennington's?" Abigail pressed.

"Er—yes," Mr. Holmes responded, ending with a wide smile, the sort that he hoped would put to rest any concerns.

"The fox are quite plentiful in these parts."

"Yes, there is nothing like a good foxhunt, being as they are such wily creatures."

"And the roe are plentiful as well—the primary reason Lord Bennington chose to purchase property here."

Ignoring the glower from Constance, Abigail turned Edwards. She now had no doubts as to who had initiated the invitation to Holmes and Edwards. Constance had always had her brother wrapped about her finger.

"And you, sir," Abigail continued. "Are you partial to the sport as well?"

"It is not my primary interest in coming," Edwards replied smoothly.

"Then what, pray, compels you here?"

He stared at her as if to say: *You.*

Abigail forced a swallow. If he was going to stare at her with such penetration the entire time, she was unsure if she could sit still.

"I hear the races here are as good as one might find at the Royal Ascot," Edwards said.

"Are you a fan of horse racing then, Mr. Edwards?"

Not to be caught in the same false step as his friend, Edwards replied, "I may not be considered a *devotee*, but that has not hindered my interest in attending the activity now and then."

"Abbey is an exceptional judge of horseflesh," Constance provided. "I have many times attempted to convince her to bet on the races for sure she would see much success."

"I take it you will be attending the races then?" Edwards asked of Abigail.

"She never misses them! Will you as well, Mr. Edwards?"

"Indeed."

Constance clapped her hands. "What delightful happenstance!"

"A truly extraordinary event," Abigail said with a raised eyebrow at Constance.

Constance cleared her throat. "Ah, the tea!"

While the tea was poured, the dialogue stayed tended towards the more innocuous topics such as the unfortunate rainclouds in the sky, the inn in town that the gentlemen were lodging at, and the vistas to be seen of the countryside. They had finished their tea when Lord Bennington arrived home. Greetings were exchanged. Mr. Holmes inquired as to the hunt. Lord Bennington replied that he had fired off a few shots, but they did not find their mark.

As the men conversed, Abigail pulled Constance aside.

"This is your doing, is it not?" Abigail whispered.

"What a thing to accuse your bosom friend of," Constance deflected.

"My only question is whether Mr. Edwards is here for your attentions or mine?"

"His preference appears to lie with you."

Abigail paused. That he might be partial to her provided some gratification, but she was too seasoned to be truly flattered.

The women took their leave to attend to their toilette while Lord Bennington guided Edwards and Holmes on a tour of the various antlers decorating his house. After changing from her riding habit to a simple but comfortable gown of muslin, Abigail headed back downstairs. She had hoped her days in Berkshire would afford a respite from the distractions of London, but she meant to put a stop to the mischief her friend intended. Constance was already with the men when Abigail found the group in the hall viewing a mounted stag's head with thirteen-point antlers.

"My most exceptional kill," Lord Bennington described. "Might easily have been he who had gotten me. Looked me dead in the eye. I think he would have charged me, but my trusty blunderbuss was quick on the draw and did lay the beast down with but one shot."

As they strolled down the hall, Lord Bennington recalled the details of every kill from the firearm used to the weather of the day. Abigail had heard the stories before and found herself sauntering near the rear of the party with Mr. Edwards.

"Do you favor hunting, Mr. Edwards?" Abigail asked him.

Though she had not taken any extraordinary pains with her dress, it seemed that Mr. Edward's eyes had lighted upon seeing her.

"I am not averse to the sport," he replied.

She eyed him carefully. "You prefer a different sort of hunt perhaps?"

He looked at her. "My lady?"

"I have inquired after you. You have quite the reputation in Bath."

He did not blink. "You flatter me, Lady Debarlow."

She raised her brows at his response. She had expected a prompt denial of the allegation or an attempt to hide some manner of smug acknowledgement.

"That I have merited such attention on your part," he elaborated.

"You do not deny it then?"

"What part of my character would you have me deny?"

Was he sincere in asking her? she wondered. Perhaps he was merely stalling, but if he was flustered, he hid it well. She glanced ahead and saw that they had fallen further back from the rest of their party.

"Your reputation as a rakehell, sir," she supplied.

He studied her as if she were the one under judgment and responded without wavering, "I do not deny that such a brand has been attached to my name."

"Justly?" she demanded. She would not allow him escape answering frankly by toying with words.

He held her gaze with his. Her heart palpitated—to her disconcertion. He should be the one flustered, not she.

"Justly."

There was no sound of shame or arrogance in how he spoke. He spoke as if stating no unremarkable fact, as if he were confirming the price of a loaf of bread. His answer did not bring her the satisfaction she had expected. At the least he was a rogue who admitted his colors.

"You have a long list of prey," she persisted.

"As long as yours, perhaps?" he returned.

Her chin went up in defense. "*Touché*. But I am not afforded so kind a term as rakehell."

"A grievous inequity," he concurred.

Abigail considered her own words. She had never considered herself a huntress in her pursuit of men, but perhaps her stripes did not differ vastly from his.

"You do not take offense at my metaphor of the hunt?"

"Would it change your perception of me? Would you not still think me an ogre who targets the unsuspecting and defenseless, then touts the sum of his preys like so many trophies he has amassed? Would you cease to advise your friends of the fair sex to stay their distance from me?"

Such advice would fall upon deaf ears, Abigail thought wryly of Constance. She could not help a small smile.

"If I had a daughter, I would counsel her to stay away from men like you," Abigail acknowledged, "but I do not know you well enough to consider you an ogre."

"Your want of prejudice is gratifying, Lady Debarlow," he bowed. "Even were you to consider me a monster, I venture to say that you would not fear me."

It was her turn to hold his gaze. "I fear no man."

The other three had stopped at the last of Lord Bennington's trophies. Abigail and Mr. Edwards attended to Lord Bennington's words as if they had been listening the whole time.

"Come, you will have supper with us," Lord Bennington declared when he had finished his tale of how he had nearly come across a moose. "I regret there will be no fresh venison on the table tonight, but perhaps if we are fortunate tomorrow…"

Abigail noted the satisfied smile upon her friend and expected that Constance would find a way to have Mr. Edwards seated next to her.

"You are generous, Lord Bennington," Edwards spoke. "But we should not trespass upon your hospitality further. I am sure the repast at the Red Cock Inn will suit us perfectly well."

"Nonsense. Please accept my invitation or I should be discouraged."

That put an end to any more objections. Lord Bennington rarely passed an opportunity to regale newcomers with this hunting exploits. Abigail wondered that Mr. Edwards would refuse dinner. Perhaps he was not completely aware of Lady Constance's plans for him. As Abigail predicted, Constance insisted Mr. Holmes sit beside her brother that they may better converse about their favorite pastime. She then sat herself beside Mr. Holmes, leaving Abigail and Mr. Edwards to sit across from them on the other side of Lord Bennington. But as his lordship dominated the dinner conversation, Abigail and Montague exchanged few words. After dinner, the men retired to the drawing room to round off the evening with brandy and tobacco.

"Has he seduced you yet?" Constance inquired of Abigail, her eyes flashing at the thought.

"Mr. Edwards, I presume?" Abigail returned as the two women enjoyed a bottle of port.

"Of course! Lest you prefer Mr. Holmes?"

"My dear, you have no shame…"

Constance tossed her curls. "For which you adore me. Come, tell me what he has done."

"He has made no effort as far as I can tell. Perhaps he did not fully comprehend your instructions?"

Constance pursed her lips. "Instructions indeed. I told him nothing."

"And you expect me to believe that?"

"How can he have made no attempts. I thought he had a repute in Bath."

"Which I had emphasized to him as well."

Constance frowned. "Abbey, you did not!"

"He took it quite well. Wasn't abashed in the faintest."

"Well, how the devil is a man to work his charms upon you if you accuse him of being a debaucher?"

Abigail laughed. "If he is indeed accomplished in the art of seduction, he will not allow that to stop him."

Constance brightened at the thought.

"But perhaps you have misread his partiality for me."

Constance shook her head. "He is biding his time—a sign of his patience—a virtue in bed. There is naught more disappointing than a lover who rushes."

"Constance, you know my mind to be set on Tremayne."

"Yes, but a small, little illicit affair of short duration could hardly hurt your campaign with the Viscount."

"I do not know Mr. Edwards well enough to trust his discretion."

"And if you could?"

Abigail sighed. "I *might* entertain his attentions, but—"

"Then that shall be my mission."

"You cannot prove him trustworthy or not."

"No, but perhaps the right incentive could be found."

"You are incorrigible!"

Constance beamed. "For which you adore me."

They sipped their port, each lost in her own thoughts for the moment. Abigail knew it to be fruitless to persuade her friend from pursuing Mr. Edwards—not with his presence so near. Perhaps it would do no harm to learn a little more about Montague Edwards.

CHAPTER SEVEN

MONTAGUE COULD NOT refrain from thinking of the Baroness—nay, from *wanting* her. Every thought of her prompted his cock to stiffen. He remembered vividly the vision of her when she had entered the Bennington drawing room, tendrils of her hair protruding chaotically, her hat askew upon her head. The disarray had only lent a more earthly quality to her appearance. The blood pulsed in his cock. In contrast to the masculine cut of the riding habit, her evening dress had emphasized the feminine properties. Once again, he had been drawn to the display of her neck and collar— territory that he wished to traverse once more.

Laying in his bed at the inn, Montague ran his hand against his shaft. Lady Debarlow had looked magnificent in both her gowns, but neither compared to what he had seen her wearing in the *Cavern of Pleasures*. He had felt an attraction to her that first night at the Bennington ball, and his witness of her at Madame Botreaux's only made her more desirable. What a wicked, wanton woman was the Baroness Debarlow! He rubbed his cock more vigorously as he imagined himself in place of the Viscount. Only he would not wish to simply stand in submission to what she wished to do.

"She is not a true dominant," Penelope had said.

"You know this to be true?" Montague had asked.

"I have witnessed her in both situations."

Montague felt his head reeling.

Penelope put a hand upon his arm. "Come, let us begin your training."

* * * * *

The mare beneath her pranced with increasing unease, and Abigail realized that she should have turned around a half hour earlier when first the horse became skittish. The mare had been reluctant to leave the comfort of her stables, but Abigail wanted to have the wind rushing at her once more, to cool her body and wash away that uncomfortable longing between her legs when she thought of Montague Edwards.

Lord Bennington had not allowed the grey clouds to stop him and his guests—Holmes and Edwards—from their hunt. Constance had declined to go for a ride, and Abigail welcomed the solitude. She did not want to spend the hour fending off her friend's crusade. The grey clouds, however, had darkened considerably and a gentle roll of thunder caused the mare to shake her head and Abigail to pull the reins tighter.

"Let us turn to home," Abigail told Andromeda with a reassuring stroke.

A few drops of rain preceded a deluge. Abigail quickened her pace, but it would do no good to rush home upon such wet grounds. A sudden flash of light followed by a clap of thunder caused the mare to rise onto her hind legs. Abigail lost hold of the reins and tumbled to the ground. The fall took the air from her and jarred her limbs. After the apex of the impact had passed, Abigail rose to her feet and looked about for Andromeda. The mare had disappeared. Abigail hoped but doubted that Andromeda had enough presence to return home. Rubbing her bruised backside, Abigail hobbled up a hill to see if she could spot Andromeda. Where could the mare have run off to?

The steady rain blanketed the countryside as far as the eye could see. Abigail dragged herself and her now sodden skirts back down the hill. There was naught to be done but to head back. When she reached the Bennington house, she felt that she was more water than human. She wiped away an endless stream of rain from her eyes. Her clothes, heavy with wetness, had made the walk home no simple matter. The mud had seeped halfway up her gown and clung to her shoes. Her white stockings and petticoats, too dirtied to be washed, would have to be tossed. She made her way to the stables, hoping to find Andromeda dry and warm. How she would laugh with relief at the wretched creature!

But her heart sank as she walked in.

The hunting party must have returned shortly before her. Mr. Holmes and Mr. Edwards were headed out of the stables as she entered. Though they, too, were soaked to the bone, they did not appear as ragged as she.

"Lady Debarlow!" Mr. Edwards exclaimed upon seeing her.

She must have looked miserable sight, but she little cared. She only noted that Andromeda was not among the horses in the stables.

"Andromeda," she said to the stable boy. "Have you seen her?"

The lad shook his head.

"Lady Debarlow, what has happened?" Mr. Edwards asked with noticeable concern.

Abigail pictured Andromeda, alone and frightened, with the rain beating down upon her and the lightening flashing above her.

"Oh, what a fool I am!" she scolded herself. "I should never have taken her out in this weather."

"Your horse?"

She nodded. "The lightening and thunder had frightened her. I fell and she fled. Where I know not. She could be anywhere. The poor, stupid animal! But it is I who am to blame. I was selfish and had insisted upon riding."

She turned to the stable boy and gestured to the grey. "Have Orses saddled. I must go in search of Andromeda."

"My lady," Edwards intervened, "you would be more fool to venture out in such conditions."

She looked out at the dark skies. "But it is my fault that she is out there."

"I cannot permit you to go."

Her chin shot up and her eyes widened. Had she heard the man correctly?

"I know your thoughts, my lady," he intercepted. "I am indelicate and audacious to make such an assertion over your will. As recompense for my offense, you will allow me to go in search of your horse."

He turned to the stable boy. "Do as Lady Debarlow bids. Have the horse saddled."

Abigail stood in silence, not knowing whether she should be indignant that he was assuming a responsibility that should have been born by her or grateful for his chivalry.

Edwards turned next to his friend. "Latimer, please see Lady Debarlow into the house."

Still undecided as to how she should react, she accepted the arm proffered by Holmes and allowed him to guide her out of the stables. She turned to see Edwards mounting the grey. With a quick spur of his legs, he urged the horse out into the pouring rain. The thunder had softened, signaling the nascent retreat of the tempest, but it would be no easy matter to find Andromeda. Now she had sent two souls out to suffer the unkind elements.

"It will take more than a storm to fell Montague," Holmes offered as if reading her thoughts.

Abigail nodded but bit upon her lower lip nonetheless. Upon entering the house, she realized how cold she felt. She went up into her room to shed her sodden garments. Seeing herself in the mirror, she saw how horrendous she looked with her hair plastered to her face and her riding habit tarnished with mud. She considered a hot bath to warm herself, but she was anxious to see when Mr. Edwards might return.

After her maid had peeled the layers of wet clothing from her, Abigail donned a simple grey muslin with black ribbons at the waist and elbows. Her maid had pinned under-ruffles beneath the sleeves and tucked an ivory colored *fichu* into the low neckline. Still feeling chilled, she wrapped a shawl about herself. She was about to slip her feet into a pair of silk brocade slippers when Charlotte burst into the room.

"What a relief you are arrived safely!" her friend exclaimed. "I was enjoying a peaceful slumber in the library when I was awoken by the thunder. "Did I not remark how ominous the skies looked?"

"I should have heeded you," Abigail acknowledged. She looked out the window to see the rain still splattering the glass.

"Mr. Holmes said that Mr. Edwards has gone out in that dreadful weather to find Andromeda?"

"I was thrown from her and she bolted away."

Charlotte rushed to her side. "My dear! Are you hurt?"

"A bit bruised but largely unharmed. I only wish I had stayed here as you did."

She paced the room, glancing out the window every few seconds to see if the storm had subsided.

Charlotte peered out the window. "That Mr. Edwards must be mad to be out in such foulness. Perhaps you are right not to mind his attentions."

"He would not have me venturing out."

Charlotte said nothing but Abigail felt her gaze.

"He is returned!" she cried, spotting a dark form through the grey of rain.

Whirling on her heels, she hurried down to the stables as Edwards approached, astride his horse, his hand holding the reins as he led Andromeda. She ran to take the mare from him.

"Forgive me," she mumbled to the horse as she rubbed its side.

"I found her wedged between the hillside and a large bush," Edwards said as he dismounted. "She would not emerge at first, but with a bag of oats, I coaxed her to me. I think she is now more wearied than fearful."

She removed the reins and harness as the stable boy undid the saddle. Once Andromeda was safely returned to her stall, Abigail turned to Edwards, who had stabled his own horse.

"I am grateful, sir," she said and let loose the sigh of relief she had been holding inside of her. "Thank you."

Despite being soaked from head to toe, he executed a bow as if they stood comfortably at a ball before a dance. "Your servant."

When he looked up, she was struck by the subtle verdant shading of his irises. How had she not noted the hue before? A strand of his hair had adhered across his forehead. Without thinking, she reached to brush it aside. He caught her wrist just as her fingers swept the forelock back in place. Her heart stopped. She could not pull her hand back, but she doubted that she could move even were he to release her from his grip. She knew what he was about to do and yet a mixture of hope and apprehension swelled within her.

He cupped the back of her neck with his other hand and tilted her head as he brought her to him in one fluid motion to capture her lips with his. Suddenly all other sensations were eclipsed by him. The smell of damp horseflesh and wet grass was replaced by the scent of him. The steady pattering of the rain outside the stables faded against the sound of her hammering heart, which had hastened from its previous standstill faster than a horse could break into a gallop. Her eyes had closed of their own volition, allowing the feel of the kiss to overwhelm all else. His mouth felt firm against her, but not overpowering—the control of one well versed in the act of kissing. His lips guided hers, and with each taste, she felt an inescapable heat pooling in her loins. While she relished his finesse, she would not have minded if he were to crush his mouth atop hers. She indicated her eagerness by her attempts to explore and taste all parts of his mouth. He responded by pulling her closer to him until she could feel the wetness of his garments. It did nothing to cool her ardor. Indeed, being pressed against his hard body only intensified the longing between her legs.

He slid his mouth down her neck, and she arched herself further into him. Against the coolness of her skin, his caress was hot enough to warm her entire body. She took the opportunity to take in a much needed breath and softly groaned at how delicious his lips felt upon her. His hand brushed aside her *fichu* to gain him access to the tops of her breasts. Drops of rain fell from his head onto her bosom. The coolness of the water mixed with his heat made her head swim. She could not recall when last she had felt such exhilaration. Desire built within her sure and fast, and she would have him rip the *fichu* from her. She grasped the lapels of his coat with both hands.

His breath had quickened as much as her own, but he abruptly pulled his head up. Had he sensed her desperation? Was he repelled by it? Should she have demonstrated more womanly reserve? There was no mistaking the hunger in his gaze, as if he meant to devour her with his eyes alone, but then why did he desist?

"I did not go in search of Andromeda to secure such an award," he said huskily.

She continued to hold his lapels and felt his arm still around her back. She did not want him to release her.

"Do you disapprove?" she asked over a shaky breath.

"Hardly. You have rightfully called me out as a roué. I would not deny it and affront your intelligence. Nor would I deny that I much desire to finish what had begun in the library at the Bennington ball. But I think, my lady, that you would rue what had transpired here."

She could not help feeling provoked by his words. She was no chit come late from the schoolroom. What manner of seducer was he?

"Pray tell you are not a rake with a conscience?" she responded.

He considered her words before answering, "A conscience would be a sorry liability for a rake."

"Indeed. And I think you underestimate which one of us is the greater voluptuary."

A muscle pulled at the corner of his mouth. "I understand your tally of lovers to exceed mine own, but I am told you are now committed to the Viscount Tremayne."

Of course. She had, perhaps conveniently, forgotten Charles. It vexed her that she should be reminded of him by Montague Edwards of all people.

"And the specter of another man has stopped you before? I wonder that you have had as much success as has been claimed?"

Her attack on his manhood had found its mark for his eyes steeled and his arm about her stiffened. She was about to be ravaged...

* * * * *

Montague had her where he wanted. The Viscount may or may not forgive her upon learning that she had lifted her skirts to another.

Regardless, Montague would have taken a significant step towards accomplishing the Earl's goal. He should, therefore, have no cause not to devour the Baroness in the manner urged by every fiber in his being save for that peculiar thing he had dismissed but moments ago—a conscience. Why that quality should rear its head after years of dormancy was baffling at best. Perhaps it was a consequence of his contempt for the Earl of Frotham.

Her lips hung deliciously close beneath his. His cock urged his body towards her. She would have fitted perfectly against him. In more ways than one, Lady Debarlow was a fitting match to him. He need not worry of the aftermath with her. There would be no tearful adieus, no attempts to form an attachment, no heart broken, no sorrow turned to spite. Theirs was a mutual understanding to satisfy the cravings of the flesh. She was as like to use him as he was of her.

But a tumble now could prove but a short term gain. He knew women well enough to know their lust could as easily wane as surge, like the ebb and flow of the menses. To fulfill his charge, he needed to woo the Baroness completely from Tremayne. For that he required a more lasting commitment. Yet, what harm could a little dalliance beget?

"The foil comes off the rapier, I see," he remarked, silently cursing his hesitation—a most unfamiliar state for him. It was true that his venture out into the damnable weather was not intended as part of his seduction. The poor woman had looked so distraught that the thought of procuring that which she most desired at the moment emboldened him. He had relished the anticipation of seeing the look of joy upon her face should he return successfully with the mare. He was not naïve and had certainly entertained the possibility that her appreciation might lend itself to deeper feelings, but he had not expected to find her waiting for him at the stables.

"Are we adversaries then, Mr. Edwards?"

He could sense the balance of power shifting. The art of seduction was a delicate dance with the movement oftentimes alternating between partners. Nonetheless, he found most women content to have the man leading the dance. It was for him a comfortable role. He had suspected, even prior to seeing Lady Debarlow at Madame Botreaux's, that she would entertain an interest in being at the helm. Her control of the situation disarmed him, but only briefly. He would allow her command for the time being.

"Only if you wish it," he answered.

She contemplated his words, and he could see her senses returning to the space formerly occupied by sensibilities. She withdrew from him, but he pulled her back to him. Her eyes widened in surprise. He had permitted her enough consideration. It was his turn once more to be the aggressor.

"I would change your mind, Baroness," he said as he moved a hand to the base of her head and recalled his caresses from that night in the library, "and bid you call a truce."

Her eyes fluttered in her attempts to fend off what his touch was doing to her, but he could feel her body melting into his. He lowered his head and kissed the collar he had been eyeing every time she wore a low décolletage. Kneading away the tension in her neck as he caressed her chest with his lips, he dismissed all doubts regarding the wisdom of his actions. He did not want to go another night wondering what it would be like to hold her. The desires of his body overruled more rational thought. To hell with the consequences. He would deal with them later. For now, he would have her.

CHAPTER EIGHT

WHAT HAD HAPPENED? Abigail wondered even as she thrilled to his touch. She had wanted him, then persuaded herself otherwise, only to find her desires enflamed once more. He had an *exquisite* embrace. She felt surrounded by his presence: one hand pressing against the small of her back, the other working its charm upon her neck, his lips searing the cool of her skin. Wrapped in his arms, she felt safe to lose herself in the passion. Perhaps it would prove a deceptive security, but his caresses were melting away all caution.

"The stable boy," she murmured against his ear when his mouth had kissed a trail up the side of her neck.

"Would his presence deter you?" he replied as he nipped deliciously at a spot behind her ear, making her rise to the tips of her toes and her concern for privacy to fade.

"I see you've no shame."

Lifting her by the waist, he whirled her around and backed her against a stable post. "None."

He pressed his body over hers. The wetness from his clothes began to seep into hers, but the dampness could not dull the fire that had started between her legs and now engulfed her whole. She groaned when he put his mouth to the angle where her neck joined her shoulder.

"Faith, I thought I had come upon my equal in the Lady Debarlow," he murmured as he tilted her chin up with his thumb and kissed the softness beneath her jaw.

Half formed questions fluttered through her head of what he might have heard to give him that supposition, but she heeded not such nuisance. She had determined that she wanted him. As delightful as his caresses were, she wanted his mouth on hers. He had teased her hunger to aching heights and would rip the clothes from him if he allowed it.

"I am shocked by nothing," she declared, "but I freely admit to possessing a shred of shame. The stable boy is not yet a man."

"We have been alone for some time," he assured.

It surprised her not that he would be aware of their surroundings—more so than she to her chagrin. She vaguely recalled a moment earlier when he had seemed to look past her and inclined his head towards the door. Perhaps that had been his directive to the stable boy to leave. He was a practiced seducer, indeed, and she was comforted to know that she was in the hands of a master.

"But our privacy is by no means certain," he pointed out, "as anyone can come upon as at any moment."

"Then why do we dally?" she responded, rolling her hips against him.

His gaze of her hardened and then his mouth descended fully upon hers. At last! she thought, savoring the ability to return his attentions. She devoured him equally, their tongues entwining as they tasted the depths of each other's mouth. She heard him groan and felt the rod between his legs pressing against her hip through her petticoats. Reaching a hand between them, she rubbed his shaft. He grunted, pulled her away from the post, and lay her down into a bed of hay. She wrapped a leg around him as he covered her body with his. Too consumed by lust, she ignored the discomfort of the hay and arched herself against his weight.

Gathering her skirts in one hand, he pulled them up to her garters, high enough for him to snake his hand beneath them. He cupped a buttock before sliding his hand around her thigh, slick with the wetness of her lush, and to the nub of flesh at her mons. He grazed it with his thumb. She gasped. Over and over he glanced his thumb across her clitoris, drawing the wetness from her until she could feel the petticoat moist beneath her arse. He circled his thumb gently on the swollen nub and ran a finger along her quim. When he had found the spot that made her moan and strain the most, he applied quicker and more forceful strokes. She wanted the penetration of his cock but could not bring herself to stop his delightful ministrations. Her voice was not her own as she emitted gasp after gasp, groaning and whimpering, whimpering and groaning. He pressed his thumb into her flesh and agitated her vigorously until she convulsed against him and a cry tore from her throat.

Somewhere a horse neighed and pawed the ground. He eased her down from her climax with gentle, languid strokes. She shuddered and took a long haggard breath as the wave of her orgasm subsided. She opened her eyes and looked into his. Was it his own unsatisfied ardor that made him gaze so intently upon her or was his look of disconcertion part of his seduction? Realizing she was clinging to his coat still, she released her grasp. She should have been satiated, but the greedy part of her wanted it all over again.

He rolled off her.

"Are we finished?" she asked, surprised, glancing at the still obvious bulge in his breeches.

He kissed her thigh and looked at her with shimmering eyes. "Only for now."

She tried not to show her disappointment. Her mind had hummed at the thought of his thick, stiff cock buried inside of her. Strange that he should not seek his own fulfillment. She did not encounter many of his sex who did not wish to eagerly relieve their hardened desires, especially after they had attended to her. Did he not desire her enough? Perhaps he needed encouragement. She reached for the buttons of his breeches, but he caught her by the wrist.

"The gesture is appreciated but unnecessary," he said as he stood and pulled her to her feet. He plucked the hay protruding from her hair.

Still a little baffled, she peered at his face for answers. "Are you in haste?"

"I must admit to wanting myself out of these damned sopping clothes."

She blinked. He was ranking dry clothing above an opportunity to spend? He must not have heard all that was said about her or he would know that no man had ever claimed her to be a poor tumble in the sack—or hay.

He picked up her shawl from the floor and handed it to her. She wrapped it about herself and put on a mask of dispassion.

"I shall be sure to call upon you, Mr. Edwards, if ever I should go riding in a storm once more," she said lightly as she took his arm.

They headed back to the house.

"I pray that you will, Lady Debarlow."

They walked the rest of the way in silence. Abbey envisioned Charlotte pouncing upon her with questions as to what had happened. For the first time, she would have to reply that she was not at all quite sure.

* * * * *

Montague felt as if he had been holding his breath for the past five hours. From the moment his lips took hers till he was ensconced back in his room at the inn, his body was tensed like a bow primed to shoot. Taking his body off of Lady Debarlow had taken an exhausting resolve. His head had spun upon finding her so wet between the legs. His cock yearned to taste the honey from her quim. But he had seen her desire and knew that he had to leave her unfulfilled that she might wish for another encounter. He had intended to ruffle her and thought he might have succeeded, though her nonchalance at the end was rather convincing.

"Would you not say that you have successfully seduced the Baroness?" Latimer inquired as they rode a carriage back to London. "I wonder what manner of proof the Earl requires?"

"I am successful only if Lady Debarlow relinquishes Tremayne or if he were to renounce her," Montague corrected.

"And which of those ends are you hoping to orchestrate?"

"Either would suffice for my purposes."

"But she has seen fit to lift her skirts to you. I should say it were no monstrous effort to induce her attentions toward you and away from Tremayne?"

Montague looked out the carriage window in thought. "I know not what compels her to Tremayne. Persuading her to lay with me is easier than penetrating her trust. Most women are more like to give first of their affections than their body, but Lady Debarlow is the reverse."

"Why worry of her affections? You have clearly spoken to her carnal desires."

"Because you cannot conquer a woman by invoking lust alone."

Latimer stretched his long legs before him. "Is that why I have failed so many times before?"

Montague smiled. "My friend, you would rather apply yourself to a round of hazard at Brooks'."

"True, true. I must say that you owe me one, Edwards. Dragging me out here to the country to suffer such godforsaken weather. Not to mention enduring that Lord Bennington and his countless stories of his battles with various beasts. Gad, you would think he had come across Goliath if he had met a canary. And I can safely declare that I loathe the sport of hunting."

The following day proved more propitious when Jonathan informed him that Lady Charlotte and the Baroness Debarlow were to ride through St. James' Square. Montague selected a pair of buff breeches, high glossed boots, and a dark blue coat. He had his steed brought round.

The warm day had brought a crowd to St. James Square, but he managed to spot the two women riding. He directed his horse toward them.

"Lady Charlotte, Lady Debarlow," he greeted with a touch of his hat.

The former gave him a wide smile, but the latter only nodded.

"Mr. Edwards, how nice to see you," Lady Charlotte returned.

"How is it that we should cross paths so frequently in so small a time, Mr. Edwards?" Lady Debarlow wondered with an eye upon her friend.

"The work of Fate, no doubt! But you, sir, have you no comment as to how lovely a picture we present upon such a fine day?"

"I am remiss," he replied. "Forgive me. I hope you would not believe that my lack of poetry or ability to offer such pleasant flattery signifies that I regard you ladies as anything but a vision."

"Mr. Edwards is not the flattering sort," Lady Debarlow observed.

"And would that be a flaw or a quality, my lady?"

"It is neither at present."

She studied him, and a cool silence fell upon them.

"Well, Mr. Edwards, you are forgiven," Lady Charlotte spoke. "I tire of men who are prone to excessive flattery."

Lady Debarlow stifled a yawn. He started. Did she find his presence boring?

Lady Charlotte, also disconcerted by her friend's response, continued, "You are to be praised, sir, for your modesty as you are quite the hero, having braved the most treacherous elements to rescue Andromeda. Do you not agree, Abbey?"

Lady Debarlow turned her attention back to them. "I, too, appreciate the modesty and had expressed my gratitude to him for his efforts."

She turned away as if in search of someone else. Clearly, she was not as committed to the *tête-à-tête* as her friend. She had been desperate and frantic to find Andromeda, but from her tone, one might have deduced that he had simply gone round the block to retrieve her bonnet. Her behavior was most unsettling and not what he would have expected from the fair sex. From a rogue, yes—one who, in the light of day, regretted having lain with the virgin and wanted no more to do with her. He found himself a little angry at the thought that she might lament their moment in the stables.

"Any gentleman would have done as much," he said.

"Hardly!" Lady Constance exclaimed.

Lady Debarlow said nothing.

"Mr. Edwards!" a voice called.

He saw Lady Evalina waving at him from an open carriage. Beside her sat the dour Lady Louisa. The company of those two ladies was far less inviting than the two before him, but he had the sense he had overstayed his welcome with the Baroness.

He touched his fingers to his hat. "It were a fine day, and I will not keep you ladies further from its enjoyment."

He turned his horse towards Lady Evalina.

* * * * *

Evaline eyed her new gown in her bedchamber mirror and was pleased to conclude that she and the dress made a perfect match. Surely the vision of her in this gown would catch the eye of Mr. Edwards? After seeing him at St. James' Square—he cut a rugged figure upon horseback—she was determined to know him better.

The sound of a horse approaching drew her to her window. It was as if Providence had read her mind for she saw none other than Mr. Edwards! She admired his form upon a horse. He had an easy but upright posture. She would not have been able to abide by a man who did not look stately upon a horse. She doubted Mr. Edwards could appear in poor form regardless. He moved with such understated confidence. He was unlike any man she had come across. The thought that he might have come to call upon her made her heart flutter. Oh, but she was not ready to be viewed!

"Quick, Maggie!" she barked at her chambermaid. "Finish pinning the gown and do not tarry. And fetch my gold slippers with the pink roses. Be quick about you!"

The maid complied. Evaline even had time to add a dash more rouge to her lips. The women in Bath, if they were pretty, surely could not present a *significantly* lovelier sight. With a satisfied sigh, she waited for the butler to knock upon the door.

"Maggie, there is a guest come to our house," Evaline directed when the knock did not materialize, "go and see what has become of him."

Unable to wait further, she followed Maggie but stayed above stairs, wanting to make a grand entrance for Mr. Edwards. She wanted to appear like an angel floating from down on high.

"Lady Evalina," Maggie said upon returning, "it appears a Mr. Edwards came to call upon His Lordship."

Evaline was disappointed but not for long. Of course the proper thing for Mr. Edwards to do was to call upon her father. But what if his purpose was not to see her?

"Where are they now?" she asked.

"In His Lordship's library."

Evaline decided she had best wander downstairs in the event that Mr. Edwards might miss his opportunity to see her. She passed by the door of her father's library and considered entering on some pretext requiring her father's attention, but she paused upon hearing the roused voice of the Earl.

"He has declared that he has no intention to marry Miss Worsely at all!" her father was saying. "The situation has worsened. Have you made no progress?"

Mr. Edwards responded in a cool, deep tenor. Not able to catch his every word, Evaline pressed her ear to the door.

"I think you must need hasten your efforts. I can assure you that Worsely will not tolerate any slights upon his daughter."

"Even were the Baroness to abandon her attentions upon your son, there is no assurance he will cooperate where Miss Worsely is concerned."

"I will worry of the latter. *You* take care of the Baroness."

Take care of the Baroness? Evaline wondered what her father could have meant.

"I have not forgotten our arrangement."

She thought she detected a perturbed note in his response and would have gathered that Mr. Edwards was not overly enamored of her father.

"Indeed. I should imagine with Chelton at stake, you would apply yourself with utmost earnest."

She wondered who or what Chelton might be. It was plain her father was agitated over Charles, but what had Mr. Edwards to do with it all? The sound of movement made her scramble from the door and back up the steps. She pretended to be walking down the stairs when Mr. Edwards emerged from the library. He was visibly disgruntled.

"Oh!" she gasped, feigning surprise. "Mr. Edwards, is it not?"

He bowed. "Lady Evalina."

Stopping a few steps above him, she presented her hand. He took it and pressed his lips near her knuckles. The warmth and strength of his grasp caused her to shiver. He must have noticed it for he glanced up at her with a more probing stare. She attempted to stymie the blush that was surely crawling up her countenance.

"What brings you here?"

"A matter of business, if you will, betwixt your father and I."

Matter of business? What a strange way to term their discussion regarding her brother's marital situation. She was still extremely puzzled as to why Mr. Edwards would be privy to such a sensitive matter of her family. She noted that he had his hat tucked beneath his arm and gloves in hand. No doubt he expected to take his leave soon.

"A simple matter, I take it, for your visit here has barely begun?" she queried.

Amusement glimmered in his eyes and she realized her error: she had revealed herself to have known of his presence despite appearing surprised.

"Are you—are you in London long?" she stammered, wishing she had not left her fan in her chambers. Her hands felt empty and idle without the ivory handled instrument.

"As long as it takes me to conclude my business here."

"I hope you are not tired of the City already?"

He smiled—it seemed especially for her. "How could I be?"

That silly maid of hers had pinned the dress too tightly for she could feel its constricting warmth right now.

"Have you taken yourself to Ranalegh Gardens yet?"

"I have not."

"They have quite the display of orchids, though I would venture that the orchids in our nursery have as beautiful a bloom. Has father shown you our gardens?"

"He has not."

Her father preferred his library and rarely ventured into the gardens, but she doubted Mr. Edwards knew that.

"My father can be quite the forgetful host. It must be nearing time for tea. Perhaps you would care to stay for tea?"

He glanced toward the closed library door, perhaps contemplating whether or not the Earl would approve of his company.

"You are most gracious, Lady Evalina, but I think it best if I decline for today."

Her lips pursed in disappointment, but she would not be daunted. She attributed his rejection to his discordant discussion with her father.

"Perhaps another time then?" she tried.

"Undoubtedly."

She said more cheerfully, "Then allow me to escort you out."

"I should be honored."

She smiled and took a purposeful misstep, tumbling down the last two steps straight into his arms. It was a risk for she might have ended up sprawled upon the floor—not an alluring image—but she doubted that a man like Mr. Edwards would fail to catch her. How glorious his arms felt about her, as if they could shield her from anything. Was it her imagination or did he hold her a second longer than necessary before setting her back upon her feet? This time she did not mind the flush in her cheeks.

"Lady Evalina?"

"How clumsy of me! The heel of my slipper must have caught the step."

His eyes began to glimmer once more and she wondered if he saw through her charade.

"They are pretty slippers indeed," he noted. "No doubt worth the occasional hazard?"

Pleased that he had noticed her slippers, she gave him her widest smile. "I see that you know the mind of the fair sex all too well."

"I have two sisters to credit. Though I lamented the lack of a brother when I was young, I appreciate all that I have learned from the women in my family."

They headed through the vestibule to the front doors.

"Vauxhall will be featuring a balloon ascent in a fortnight's time," she said. "Perhaps if you are not attending to your *business* matter, you could enjoy the display."

"Will Lady Evalina be in attendance?"

"I plan to be there."

"Then I shall make an effort."

Her heart quickened its beat and she could not bridge a rejoinder. He bowed over her hand before taking his leave. His horse awaited him outside and she watched as he replaced his hat and mounted the steed.

He touched his hat. "Adieu, Lady Evalina."

With her breath still caught in her throat, she could only give a curt nod. She could not wait a fortnight before she saw Mr. Edwards. There had to be a way to encounter him again—soon.

CHAPTER NINE

I T HAD BEEN YEARS since her body had experienced such divine agitation, and the hunger, once woken, would not be easily tamed. Abigail had attended to herself every night since her encounter with Montague in the stables, but she could not replicate his sweet torture. She came but the satisfaction was short-lived. She yearned for his touch. He had shown her the depth of his skills as a lover, and she would have returned the favor. Why did he not permit it? That she could not understand lest it be a tactic of his.

"There is no sense making yourself mad over it," she told herself before donning her mask and walking out into the assembly of the *Cavern of Pleasures.*

But she had felt nothing but agitation whenever she recalled what had transpired between her and Montague. He was a distraction, pulling her focus away from Tremayne. Her plans with Charles remained unfinished, and she fueled her agitation into renewed energy for her efforts with the Viscount. She had to trap him once and for all before any new obstacle presented itself. Striding into her alcove, she found the naked Viscount at his knees.

"Mistress," he greeted her. "The days have been an eternity without you. Where had you gone?"

"A submissive does not ask such questions. I go where I will and have no obligation to alert you."

"Is it wrong to profess that I have missed you?"

She could sense the Viscount to be upset. He could not have possibly known what had transpired at Lord Bennington's, and she wondered what could have prompted his distress.

"My dear, you are troubled. What has happened?"

"May I speak freely, Mistress?"

"You may."

"Very little has happened, and that be the rub. I have been obedient and patient, yet still you are distant. What more must I do?"

"You must show me in no uncertain terms your full devotion."

"But I have!" he protested.

"It is not enough for you to attend to my commands when we are here, secluded from others and shrouded in anonymity."

"But you have unmasked me here."

"The patrons here observe a code and are unlikely to reveal you."

"Then I know not what more I can do."

His complaint and self-piteous tone vexed her. "Then we are at an impasse and should discontinue our association."

She walked out of the alcove, her heart pounding. Perhaps she should not forsake Tremayne so readily, but her impatience had ruled before she could think more clearly.

"Mistress, wait!"

Tremayne came upon her and grasped her arm—most inappropriate for a submissive.

"You question my devotion, but you must know that I want you above all else."

"How?" she returned. "You are aware that I have been with many men. I find they will use all manner of words, profess all forms of adoration, but in the end, I have found naught to distinguish one from the other."

She attempted to extract her arm. A few of the other patrons near them were eying them and she did not wish to be a spectacle. But Tremayne maintained his hold.

"Has any of them asked for your hand?"

She paused, unsure if she had heard him correctly.

"Have they asked for your hand as evidence of their devotion?"

She narrowed her eyes. "Are *you* asking for my hand?"

He abruptly dropped to his knees. "If you would have me, Mistress."

Her pulse drummed in her ears as she stared down at the Viscount. It was what she had been striving for. "Your father would never approve."

"Then we head to Gretna Green. If you meet me at the Inn of Four Knights outside of London tomorrow night, I will have a carriage waiting for us."

She was tempted to question if he meant what he said, but he appeared to be in earnest.

"Very well," she said carefully. "I shall attend to my bags then."

He rose to his feet. "Do I not merit a reward for my demonstration of devotion?"

"We have yet to make it to Gretna Green." She trailed her finger along the ridge of his pectoral. "But I assure you that when we are bonded to one another, you will receive your just desert."

As she walked away, she saw the Marquess of Danforth watching her. She wondered if she had ruined her prospects with him when she was wed to the Viscount. Or her prospects with Montague. She doubted Montague would allow so trivial a thing as matrimony to hamper his efforts if he truly wished to seek her. But such things should not concern her. She was to have her vengeance upon Frotham at last. And Libby would have hers, albeit posthumously.

She happily imagined the look upon the Earl's face when he discovered his son had run off to Gretna Green with the Lady Debarlow. She would be the Viscountess Tremayne. What a lark! Charlotte would not find it nearly so amusing, but her friend would be happy to know that with Tremayne secured, she could turn her attentions elsewhere. Tremayne would no doubt accuse her of *crim con* but the damage would be done. The dye of shame would have been cast. A public divorce would only bring further scandal to the family.

She felt a nudge of pity for Tremayne, but she quelled her conscience. She deserved this. Her mother deserved this. At long last her grief would find solace. Nothing would deter her from reaching

Gretna Green.

* * * * *

"She is headed to Gretna Green with Tremayne," Jonathan informed Montague, who sat at his writing table having just finished reading an invitation from a Countess he barely knew. He expected it to be the work of Evaline Pettington.

"That is a serious development," Montague replied. "Are you sure?"

"Her maid confirms she is packing her valise. She departs tonight for the Inn of the Four Knights."

Montague put hand to jaw in thought. If they married, his objective would have failed. Even if an annulment could be procured, Frotham would not have his daughter wed the likes of Tremayne after such a scandal. He considered informing the Earl, but what could the man do but have his son kept under lock and key? It was clear the man had no powers of persuasion with his son. He could send his son off to America perhaps, but the Viscount had already shown a rebellious will of his own and was not likely to submit to his father. He could not identify anyone that Tremayne respected enough to listen to.

What did the Baroness gain by marrying the Viscount? She had lain with him but a few days before and now she wished to marry Tremayne? Was it guilt over what had happened that had prompted so extreme a step? Was she troubled by the thought of entertaining two possible lovers? He did not think it to be the case because he did not believe her affections for the Viscount to be deep enough. Perhaps if he took the Baroness into his arms once more, he could convince her to abandon the idea of marrying Tremayne. But time was of the essence.

Jonathan shook his head. "A disastrous development."

"Not yet," Montague replied, his thoughts still turning. "The first step is to ensure they do not make it to Gretna Green."

He considered what obstacles they could throw in the pair's path.

"We could pose as highwaymen and stop their coach," Jonathan offered.

"And risk having our heads blown off?"

"The Earl could send men after his son."

"And then? Lock Tremayne in a cellar until he is old and grey?"

Tremayne was evidently more attached to the Baroness than anyone had anticipated.

"Aye, if we were to inform the Earl, he might claim to have resolved the problem on his own and forego our recompense. Would the Earl allow us to shoot the Viscount in the leg? Tremayne would be incapable of travel and would require time to heal."

Montague laughed. "It were not a terrible proposal, but let us consider a few more possibilities."

It was unfortunate the Viscount had proposed, Montague thought. His efforts with Lady Debarlow had been promising of late. With more time, he could have turned her attentions away from Tremayne. If only he could have her alone for as long as he desired…

"One cannot wed without the bride," he said aloud.

"Eh?"

"Tremayne cannot marry the Baroness if she is not there."

"But it would seem she intends to go with him to Gretna Green."

"We will simply prevent that."

"How?"

"By kidnapping the Baroness."

Jonathan mulled the idea and nodded. "You are ever the clever man."

"Come, let us pack our own valise and take ourselves to this Inn of the Four Knights."

* * * * *

Abbey looked over at the young couple sitting at the table across the room from her at the Inn of the Four Knights. They huddled near each other and spoke in hushed tones, not wanting to draw notice. Every now and then she could espy their faces, though the young man wore his hat and the young woman kept the hood of her cape wrapped about her. They glanced about themselves frequently as if anticipating that the king's army might descend upon them at any moment. They also looked often at each other with a glow that could only come from love. No doubt, like she, they were headed to Gretna Green, but for quite different reasons.

Turning away from them, Abbey opened her snuffbox and inhaled a pinch of snuff. Watching the young couple made her feel old. Nor did she like the stirring of envy in her bosom. She had never experienced the purity, the optimism, the euphoria, of young love. Theirs might not be an easy life. Their parents might have disowned them. Society might shun them. But they had thrown all these considerations to the wind for the chance to be together. Without standing, theirs might be a life of poverty or hardship and certainly not the life of luxury enjoyed by the Baroness Debarlow. Abbey had oft considered herself fortunate. She had married a man she regarded with friendship and affection, and, albeit by a pained and arduous road, she had arrived at a place where she suffered for no one and was at the mercy of none. Yet, for a brief moment, she thought she might forsake all that for a taste of what the young couple had.

Despite herself, she glanced back at the couple and observed that they had but one cup between them. The young man cut into an apple and gave the young woman the larger of the slices, reserving only small bites for himself. Abbey motioned for the innkeeper and pressed a shilling into his hand.

"See that they have a bottle of wine and serve them a meal of bread, cheese, and meatpie," she instructed.

The innkeeper nodded. Rising to her feet, Abbey decided to step outside that she would not be enticed to think more about the young couple. She wanted no reservations staying her from going to Gretna Green with the Viscount. She would be a fool and have lain waste all her efforts if she did not now see her plan through. Imagine the consternation of Frotham when she and Tremayne returned to London as man and wife! Once married, she reminded herself, she and

Tremayne would lead separate lives. She would be free to pursue other interests…and other men.

The inn had very little posting traffic this time of night. Charles must have chosen this hour to minimize the chance that he might be spotted. She noted a carriage pulling up to the inn, but it had no lantern to illuminate it. Was Charles so overcome with caution that he would not allow his driver any light? The sound of footsteps behind her made her turn her head, but before she could see who it was, something was pulled over her head, blinding her. Her cry of surprise was muffled by a hand about her mouth. She grabbed at the hand and felt herself lifted off her feet and thrown onto the floor of a vehicle—likely the dark carriage she had observed. She clawed and kicked, but her arms were pinioned and her wrists bound together. Her foot connected with her assailant's body, but he only grunted before forcing her ankles together.

What a fool she was to have ventured outside the inn alone! She should have had her footman with her. Now she had been abducted by highwaymen! But why did they not simply take her jewels and her reticule? Did they intend to ransom her? Perhaps they had assumed from her attire—a tight fitting redingote with bust draping and ruffled sleeves, ribboned hat, and buckled ankle boots—that she came from a family of means. Little did they know that she had no family.

Despite being bound, she thrashed about and screamed in the hopes that someone might hear. But the carriage had lurched forward, and she could feel herself being taken from the inn. Charles would see that something had happened to her. The innkeeper would explain that she had been sitting inside the inn but a few moments ago. Charles would then go in search of her. But what if he did not arrive at the inn in timely fashion? He knew better than to keep her waiting long but what if he had been waylaid? God only knew what her abductors might do to her in the meantime. She had to escape!

"You need not worry, Baroness," a man's voice whispered above her. "You will come to no harm."

Baroness? He knew who she was then. But that was not a difficult deduction as anyone could have asked the servants her identity.

"I cannot breathe," she said.

At first, she heard no response. Then the fabric about her head was rolled above her mouth and the point of her nose.

"I would advise you to release me," she said. "Or you will have the force of Viscount Tremayne upon you."

Did she hear the man snort?

"He will discover me missing for he is expecting to find me waiting for him at the Inn of Four Knights."

"I think not for he received a note from you earlier that you have reconsidered the matter and have decided you cannot marry him."

His words stunned her. How had he known of their plans? This was the hand of the Earl at play. No one else would have an interest in what was to happen.

"What do you intend with me?" she asked carefully, wondering how far the Earl would go to prevent her from running his son.

"That shall be revealed in due time."

"Charles will not believe the note and come in search of me," she tried.

"Perhaps. If he is not devastated by your rejection and seeks verification from your lips, he will be hard pressed to find you."

A shiver shot up her spine. Did the Earl intend that Charles should never see her again? Would Frotham go so far as to have her eliminated permanently?

As if reading her mind, her abductor reminded her, "I assure you that you will come to no harm."

"You will forgive me if I do not accept your word without doubt," she replied wryly. Despite the desperate thudding of her heart, she would not cower before him. She would not give Frotham that satisfaction.

She heard him moving, then felt herself being lifted off the floor and onto the cushioned seat of the carriage. She felt his breath upon her cheek. His mouth was near her ear.

"I will amend my statement. No harm will come to you—if you abide by my commands."

"And if I do not?"

"Each act of defiance will merit a commensurate punishment."

"Such as?"

"You will discover in due time."

"I thought I was to come to no harm if I did as told?"

"Baroness, you do not strike me as the obedient sort. Nonetheless, you shall be tamed."

Her eyes widened. Good God, who was this man? What did he intend?

"You need not fear. Quite the contrary. There is much to anticipate. If I have your full and complete obedience, you shall be rewarded—with unlimited pleasures."

CHAPTER TEN

S HE WONDERED IF he could hear her heat beating. After a difficult swallow, Abbey asked flippantly, "Did Frotham issue such orders to you? I had always suspected him to be the deviant."

She felt him move across the carriage to the seat opposite her. If she could maintain a lighter tenor, her abductor might be more apt to talk.

"You speak with such venom. I take it you are not enamored of His Lordship."

So the man knew the Earl, as she had suspected. The abductor was no commoner. That much could be concluded by his speech. But why would the Earl hire a gentleman to execute his plans? Perhaps Frotham trusted this man.

"I am no friend of his," she phrased. "Whatever he is paying you, I will offer you double."

Silence.

Encouraged, she added, "I am a woman of great wealth—worth far more alive than dead."

"I have no intention of killing you," he said with an odd hitch in his voice. "I am aware of your affluence, but I think you do not know the full extent of your worth."

"Ten thousand pounds," she spat. "He offered me ten thousand pounds if I would stay away from his son. A paltry sum for all the pain…I doubt he offered you as much?"

"Why do you presume the Earl is involved?"

"Because I know his motives. He would attempt much to protect his precious son from me."

"You believe there would be no other cause for abducting you?"

"You may wish to ransom me, sir, but I have no family and no friends to whom you could address the request. But return me safely and I will assure you a most satisfying compensation."

"Define 'satisfying.'"

She thought for a moment. She had just dubbed ten thousand pounds as paltry. The amount would have to be significant to give him pause.

"Twenty thousand pounds," she pronounced. Surely the miserly Frotham could not have offered better.

His silence confirmed her assumption.

"But setting you free would not be nearly as pleasurable," he drawled.

Did her ears deceive her? Had the man refused twenty thousand pounds?

"Twenty thousand pounds," she repeated. "I jest not."

"Nor do I."

"You may have the payment in any form that you wish. Your anonymity can be maintained if you worry of retribution or reprisal."

He leaned in. "I have in my carriage and at my will a beautiful woman. A woman whose delectable body calls for the touch of man—a proper man. A woman who can ignite the deepest desires in a man with a simple glance. You would have me set free such a prize?"

Her mouth went dry. Was the man in earnest? Or was he attempting to extract a higher amount from her?

"I would consider an amount greater than twenty thousand," she offered, her voice beginning to waver for the first time.

She heard him settling back into his seat. "You may offer any sum you wish, Baroness. Would the price of your freedom be less tomorrow?"

She paled as she realized the implications of what he said. At present, he held all the cards.

"I doubt it would it change if I released you today or a sennight hence," he confirmed. "Lest you decide that you would rather not be free."

Now the man was speaking nonsense. Although...he gave every indication of being of sound mind. Though he did not seem sinister, there was clearly a malicious bent in his purpose.

"How were that possible?" she inquired, hoping to elicit more of his intentions.

"All will be revealed, Baroness, in good time."

She sensed he was done talking, and she did not pursue the matter. What could she do? What could she offer the man to reconsider his plans? Surely the Earl wanted only to keep her from marrying the Viscount. This other purpose voiced by her abductor must be of his own doing. He had seemed interested in her offer, but did he intend to rape her first before setting her free? She could offer him more if he released her unscathed, but as he had alluded, she was in no position to set the terms. Her only option was to escape at all cost.

* * * * *

Montague knew from the silence that Lady Debarlow to be contemplating her options, much as he was doing. He had been tempted to accept her offer. He would have preferred to do business with her over the Earl. He could have his twenty thousand pounds, set her free, and have no more obligations to Frotham. But he could not in good conscience exact such a grand sum from her when her predicament was not of her doing. Nor could he guarantee that Henry would sell him back the promissory notes.

She had shown an impressive presence of mind given her current situation, but he could sense her trepidation in the tenseness of her body. He wanted to put her at ease.

"In an hour we will come upon a posting inn where you may stretch your legs," he explained, "and partake of libations. I do not intend for this journey to be of great discomfort."

"Where are we headed?" she asked.

"That shall remain a mystery to you."

"And your purpose for taking me there?"

He grinned. He was looking forward to being back at Chelton, but with Lady Debarlow, the prospect was beyond inviting.

"I promise that, with good behavior, you shall be rewarded with pleasure."

"And you know that which would please me?"

Her challenge did not surprise him. "I know what pleases the fair sex."

Despite the darkness, he thought he saw her brows arch skeptically.

"A bold and overarching statement."

"Allow me to rephrase for it is true that each woman has tastes unique to herself, each possessing her own sensitivities. I know *how* to please the fair sex."

"How?"

She was curious. A good sign. He could sense a shade less fear.

"By making, as you were quick to call attention to, no assumptions and to allow her responses to dictate what I do. It were as if each woman be a new instructor, a new subject, and I always the pupil."

"You have made a 'study' of bedding a woman."

"Have you not done the same with your lovers? Discovered that which makes them mad with lust and exploited that knowledge?"

"You know my lovers?"

"I know of them. Your *liaisons* are hardly secret, though your choice of lovers is a bit mystifying."

"Indeed?"

It were probably best that he err on the side of reserve, but the question was too tempting.

"A pup like the Viscount Tremayne is hardly worth a woman of your pedigree, shall we say?"

"Polite society would not see it as you have stated."

"Polite society does not properly value a woman like yourself."

He could sense she was taken aback.

"You voice a most heterodox belief, sir. Do you purport to know me well?"

"Well enough."

"How long have you known me?"

"You are trying to discern my identity, Baroness."

"Do you fear to reveal yourself to me?"

"Do you not find the anonymity more engaging?"

"You have not answered my question: do you fear to reveal yourself?"

He could not help but smile. She was persistent.

"Not fear, Baroness. But would you not agree that it would be foolhardy of me to do so?"

"I promise that I shall not seek retribution, if you would set me free."

"I think not."

As she once more lapsed into silence, he wondered that he could restrain himself until they arrived at Chelton. He could not sit in the confines of the carriage without brushing against her skirts. Picturing her in her smart outfit, her lovely arms bound behind her, he wanted very much to take her then and there. But if he made an attempt now, she would fight him with all her might. He needed to tame the caged animal first.

They reached the outskirts of a small village. The carriage stopped in front of an abandoned old lean-to. Jonathan, who had been riding with the driver, leaped off and assisted Montague with the Baroness. She resisted at first, but feeling a pair of hands upon each of her arms, she realized that a struggle would be futile. They led her inside and sat her in a wooden chair. Jonathan fetched a lamp and placed it on the table, one of the few pieces of furniture remaining in the shelter. He laid out wine, bread, and cheese.

Montague took the only other chair sat in the darkest corner of the room. He placed his mask over his head and nodded to Jonathan to remove the Baroness' covering and bindings. Lady Debarlow winced at the light, but she quickly took in her surroundings. She looked at

Jonathan, but he was headed out the door. They heard the carriage leave.

"He will return after he has secured a fresh pair of horses," Montague supplied.

"Then it be but you and I here?" she asked, peering into the corner.

"Aye, but there is no need to entertain thoughts of escaping."

He rose from his chair and went to pour a glass of wine for her. She eyed him as if looking through his mask.

"I have seen you before," she said.

He held the glass out to her. Still in thought, she took it from him but did not drink.

"At *Madame Botreaux's*."

He paused before acknowledging, "I am gratified that my presence drew your notice."

"And apparently mine yours."

"From the very first day."

"But how is it you know who I am?" she inquired with some agitation. "Did Penelope reveal me?"

"You know she would not."

"Then how…?"

"I have other means."

He could tell from her frown that she did not like the situation.

"Fear not," he assured her. "Your identity is safe with me. I have no cause to brandish your patronage of *The Cavern* to anyone."

"Forgive me if I doubt the motives of a man who resorts to kidnapping women!"

"*Touché*. I can offer you no proof, only a promise that I have no interest in blackmailing you."

"You have abducted me simply because you were so taken by me?" she inquired with a wry smile.

He stepped towards her and leaned in. "Remarkably so."

"Your approach is rather barbaric. Do you also club women about their heads before dragging them into your cave?"

"Does the thought titillate you? Despite our evolution and our ability to engage in higher thought, man is still guided by his basest instincts. I warrant the fair sex would prefer a man who can claim his woman in no uncertain terms."

"And you are such a man?"

"Are you not here with me now?"

She smiled coyly up at him, and he felt himself drawn into her, wanting to press his lips to hers and taste her mouth once more. It seemed she turned her chin upwards to receive his kiss, but as he bent further, she threw the contents of her wine glass in his face. When he had wiped the wine from the eyes of his mask, he saw her headed for the door. He dashed towards her, knocking over the lamp in the process. The sound of it crashing to the ground made her glance back. He caught her just as she turned to open the door. She tried to jerk her arm free from him, then struck at his head. The blow nearly knocked his mask askew, but he grabbed her other wrist before she could attempt another strike. He pulled her back towards the table. She dug in her heels, but when that proved fruitless, she resisted by falling off her feet. He could have dragged her along the floor, but not wanting to wrench her arms, he hauled her up and threw her over his shoulder. She kicked and thrashed. The point of her boot caught his thigh. He contained an oath and attempted to deposit her back into the chair. However, she had managed to push her body up and clawed at his mask. She slipped off his shoulder when he fended off her attack, but he caught her as her feet touched the ground and bent her over the table. Grabbing the rope that had bound her before, he tied her arms once more behind her back. It was no easy matter for she continued her struggles, and she was no weakling. He hoped that Jonathan would not be long with the horses. He had to press her down with his weight to keep her from moving as he bound her wrists between their bodies.

"Well, Lady Debarlow," he said when he was satisfied that he had subdued her enough, "that was certainly not the obedience that I seek. And now I shall have to punish you."

Her body made a last attempt at resistance, and he felt her derriere against his thigh. His cock stirred.

"Greatly," he added as he straightened and pulled her to her feet. If he had maintained their position, he would have been too tempted to take her then and there against the table. Nonetheless, he made a note to secure a table of similar height at Chelton.

He pushed her down into the chair. Their skirmish had caused her to take in deeper breaths, and he watched the rhythmic rise and fall of her bosom for a moment.

Damn. The situation was all too intoxicating. He had never had to resort to such tactics before to seduce a woman.

"You should reconsider my generous offer," she said between breaths. "The consequences will prove dire for you elsewise."

"I see that my words continue to fall upon deaf ears. You are not the source of funds for me but, rather, of *pleasure.*"

"I do not believe you. There are far prettier women you could have abducted."

"Indeed, they are as plentiful as flowers in a garden. There is but one Lady Debarlow. I suggest you forget all attempts to escape, bribe, or threaten. And simply enjoy what is about to be done to you."

CHAPTER ELEVEN

ABIGAIL FOUND IT HARD to swallow. Who was this man? To gain entry into the *Cavern, h*e must have been someone Penelope trusted, or was impressed by. It was common knowledge that the proprietress had an eye for beauty. Abigail did not think her abductor was long a patron of *Madame Botreaux's*, but she had noticed the man in Penelope's exclusive balcony. He had somehow penetrated her inner sanctum. The man must have been handsome indeed.

Would it be possible to, as he had suggested, take pleasure in her abduction? He had foiled her moment of glory, or at least delayed it. Tremayne could hardly reproach her for having been kidnapped on the way to meet him. She would explain the extraordinary circumstance, he would be relieved to find her safe, and he would determine that instead of requiring her to meet him at some posting inn outside of London, they should travel together. It would not matter what had been written upon that forged note once she exposed the truth to Tremayne and once she had been set free. When she was to be set free. She wondered how long her abductor intended to keep her. Surely he intended to set her free at some point? Or did he plan to enslave her in some secret harem of his?

Her offer of twenty thousand pounds had interested him. She was sure of it. He was only biding his time. He meant to toy with her at first, perhaps hoping to exact more from her. She looked at him, but the lamp had rolled beneath the table, and she saw only shadows upon his face. His hair was powdered and his hands gloved. She could discern nothing from his ordinary garments. He was a gentleman, but she could find no distinguishing features. His voice was somewhat familiar, but that was likely because she had encountered him at *Madame Botreaux's*.

The sound of a carriage approaching outside drew both their attention. The door opened and another man walked in. This time she noticed the man to be in service, perhaps a footman. He appeared surprised to find the lantern upon the ground but said nothing. He retrieved the light and packed up the victuals.

"Have you any water to quench my thirst?" she asked. If there were a means to delay them…she would surely be better off here within proximity of others than wherever they intended to take her.

The footman glanced at his master, who nodded. A canteen was produced and held to her lips. As she drank the water, she wondered if there was a way to leave evidence that she had been here. It were not entirely improbable that Tremayne might discover the note to be a hoax and come in search of her.

"I am hungry," she pronounced.

"Perhaps you should have thought of it before your little act of defiance," her abductor replied. "But your punishment does not entail starvation."

He gestured to his servant, who unpacked the bread and cheese.

"I shall require my hands to eat."

"I fear you have lost that privilege, but my valet can feed you."

She bristled. She was to be fed like an animal or a child? But the thought of her hands bound behind her inspired an idea. She would leave behind one of her gloves if she were able to extricate one.

"Very well," she consented.

The valet broke off a piece of the bread and held it to her mouth. She chewed slowly. All the while her abductor watched with a faint smile upon his lips. Behind her back, she tugged at one of her gloves. It would be but a small chance that Tremayne would come across it, but it was better than naught.

The valet offered her the cheese, but she shook her head. "I have not enough of an appetite to be of further spectacle."

Her abductor pulled her to her feet and guided her out. She dropped her glove behind her before climbing into the carriage. Her abductor sat across from her once more. He crossed one leg over another.

"Let us review a few rules," he said, "that I am sure will be familiar to you. First, you are to address me always with a deferential 'Sir' when speaking. Second, you will ask permission for everything. You are to begin each request with 'Please, Sir, may I.'"

A tremor went down her spine. She was indeed familiar with such rules as they were employed by the masters at *Madame Botreaux's* as well as herself.

"Third, you shall thank me for all that I grant and all that I do. Is that understood?"

Abigail contemplated her response. She would have happily played the submissive were the master the likes of the Marquess of Danforth, but to capitulate to a stranger who had the audacity to kidnap her...

"Is that understood?" he repeated with an edge.

"Yessss," she replied reluctantly.

"Yes?"

"Yes, sir."

"I must remind you that you have a punishment forthcoming. I would not compound it were I you."

Trying not to be too irked, she ventured, "What is the nature of my punishment? Sir."

"Let us reserve that as a pleasant surprise. I will reiterate that good behavior will be rewarded, and I should prefer to mete out rewards than punishment."

"And what is your experience as a master, pray? It is no small responsibility to take on a submissive."

He waited patiently until she realized she had neglected a crucial word.

"Sir," she added grimly.

"Baroness, you are not off to a promising start."

"Surely you would allow me some reprieve as I have been put into most exceptional circumstances, Sir."

"I would for an ordinary person, but you, Lady Debarlow are hardly ordinary."

"You flatter me. Sir."

Ignoring her acerbic tone, he continued, "Therefore, I have no qualms of holding you to the highest standards. I am confident you will quickly fall in line—and enjoy doing so."

She gave a short snort.

"I see that I have quite the wayward child upon my hands," he said, his tone turning ominous. I had not expected to play the role of taskmaster so soon. Turn over."

Had she heard him correctly?

"Pardon?"

There was only scant light from the moon and stars, but she saw him shaking his head.

"Sir," he supplied.

She sucked in her breath. Damn. It had been too long since she had been in the role of the submissive. "Forgive me, sir."

"You are forgiven this once. Now turn over."

"But you—"

"I will not tolerate your insolence, Baroness."

"I—"

"I expect you to obey swiftly and without question."

She could tell from his tone that he was serious. "Turn over? Sir?"

"Turn over and kneel upon the floor."

She considered playing dumb, but that would only irritate him. Complying, she turned to face her seat and dropped to her knees. He put a hand between her shoulder blades and bent her over the seat.

For a moment she wondered if he would force himself upon her, but the dominants at Madame Botreaux's were not ravishers. Nonetheless, it were possible that a miscreant had slipped in. Her abductor had declared that no harm would come to her. He need not have made such an assurance, lest it were the truth.

"What can one do to discipline an errant child?" he queried.

"I have no children and cannot speak to what methods work best, Sir," she answered.

"My governor would take the paddle to my arse."

She became aware that her own rump faced her abductor.

"Tell me: what form of punishment do you favor, Baroness?"

"To administer or to receive, Sir?"

"I have seen you, as mistress, wield the crop often."

She heard the sound of something slicing through air and smack against flesh—his hand, perhaps. Her pulse began to throb.

"It be a favored tool of mine, Sir," she acknowledged.

"Have you felt the sting of a crop?"

She forced a swallow. "Aye. Sir."

"Did you enjoy it?"

"It would depend upon the man who held the crop, Sir."

"That was not my question, Baroness."

"I enjoyed it, Sir."

"You have used one quite extensively with the Viscount."

What was his purpose in stating such a fact? She shifted uncomfortably against the seat. She had to crane her head for it pressed flush against the back of the seat.

"How ironic then if you were to feel that same crop upon your own body."

"Do you imply that you have in your possession my riding crop? Sir."

He propped a foot next to her and slapped the crop against his boot. "It were an appropriate instrument for an equestrian."

She kept her tone light but could not resist, "You are a thief as well as a kidnapper, Sir."

"You may have your riding crop back when we are finished."

His words encouraged her. There was to be an end to their charade.

"Now, how best to address your earlier impertinence?" He tapped the crop against his boot in thought. "The possibilities are endless…and delicious."

He had patience, she allowed. In contrast, Tremayne would have thrown her skirts above her hips long before. She admired—grudgingly—how this stranger had drawn out the expectation, augmenting her agitation through his procrastination.

"Perhaps a good spanking were in order," he declared.

A mixture of uneasy emotions swirled in her stomach. She did not think she would like to be touched by this stranger, but she could not deny a small sense of curiosity and anticipation.

"The rope about your wrists will be untied," he continued. "You will lift your skirts for me…and expose your rump."

Her heart pounded more boldly. She wondered if she should speak and persuade him not to continue, but perhaps it were best to conclude this first reprimand sooner rather than later. She could certainly handle a simple spanking. She felt the tap of the crop against her flank.

"The backside of a woman is a most engaging part. As with the bosom, the curves of the buttocks are distinctive of the female sex. Both sets of orbs present such supple visions, such feasts for the eye. The body of a woman is quite balanced in that respect."

He spoke in a whisper still, but occasionally his voice would drop into a seductive baritone.

"How tempting would you consider your arse, Baroness?"

"Sir?"

"As luscious as two ripened peaches in the summer?"

"I have had little occasion to view mine own arse, Sir."

"No? That will have to be remedied, especially if you prove to have an exceptional piece. Has no one commented upon your rump before?"

"Not that I can remember, Sir."

"Describe your bum."

"I said I have had little occasion—"

"What can I expect to behold?"

"Two buttocks, Sir, lest I have grown another that I am unaware of."

"A shame we have such little illumination. I should wish to inspect your *derrière*. Perhaps we could halt the carriage and access the lantern by the driver. I think the driver and my valet would readily give their thoughts on the quality of your rump as well."

It was bad enough that she might have to bare herself to her abductor, but the thought of herself exposed to three strange men was too much.

"What do you wish for me to say, Sir?" she inquired.

"The truth. I have seen all manner of posteriors. Some are rather flat. Others bulbous like tomatoes bursting on the vine."

"I should think mine of middling size and shape, Sir."

"Is that all?"

"I do not perceive it to have any distinguishing features."

"Modesty becomes you not, Baroness."

She felt her cheeks burning at the degradation of having to discuss her arse if it were a slice of meat being sold at market.

"Do you like your arse?"

"I have an attachment to it, being as it is the only one I have owned. Sir."

"Do you exalt or despair its qualities?"

"Exalt, Sir."

"Much better. What would you say to entice attention to it?"

She envisioned her own backside and did her best to answer him. "You would find its complexion as smooth and soft as that of babe. Its appearance is full and round."

"Would one orb fit nicely in my hand?"

"Yes, Sir."

"Does it quiver when struck?"

"Most delectably, Sir."

She felt warm in the confines of the carriage—perhaps the consequence of having had to remain in her awkward position at length...or something else.

"I look forward to making an acquaintance with your bottom, Lady Debarlow. You may resume your seat."

His directive surprised her. After all that dialogue, she had expected more to come of it. Was she disappointed or relieved?

He assisted her back into a sitting position when it became clear she was having difficulty moving as the carriage jostled along the road. Her limbs were stiff, and her neck ached.

"We have a considerable length before reaching our destination," he explained. "I recommend you rest. You have before you a long venture."

She settled into her seat but doubted she could sleep.

CHAPTER TWELVE

HER EYES WERE CLOSED, but Montague could not tell if she truly slept. He unloosened his constraining cravat. He could not refrain from imagining himself fucking the Baroness in the carriage. He had taken a woman before in a carriage, and it was no easy matter given the unpredictable motions of the vehicle. But Lady Debarlow had been positioned perfectly, her rump within such easy access…

He took in a deep breath. He had been tempted to soothe her sore limbs, but that would only fuel the already uncomfortable ardor he was feeling. There would be time enough for him to show her his compassion. Too soon and she may presume his concern to be a weakness. He had one chance to convert her mind by compelling her body. To show her what she denied herself by remaining with Tremayne. It was farfetched plan, but he had not the luxury of time.

The carriage bumped along rougher roads, and Montague wished they traveled with the sunlight that he and the Baroness could witness the bucolic surroundings as they neared Chelton. Although Lady Debarlow kept her London residence for most of the year, her maidservant had told Jonathan that her ladyship did return to the country seat once or twice a year. He had had heard the estate to be quite impressive, but there was much to appreciate about Chelton.

The home where Montague had spent a happy childhood, whilst his mother lived and before he had been sent off to school after her death, had once been a small Norse castle. It was not entirely certain how his great grandfather had come into the estate save that Chelton might have been payment for a debt owed the elder Mr. Edwards. How ironic that Chelton was now the means to pay off a debt once more, Montague thought grimly.

The structure had been rebuilt a number of times in the course of its existence. Montague remembered his grandmother complaining about the draftiness of the place and questioning the wisdom of retaining the old property instead of selling it to the first bidder. His grandfather had hoped to cease her complaints by erecting a wing— built with wood instead of stone—especially for her. He had pledged Chelton to secure the funds necessary to complete the project, and thus began the first set of debts to be owed by the Montague family.

The cellar and kitchens, however, remained of stone construction and much as they were before. As did the few chambers below ground that Montague and his sisters speculated once served as dungeons. They had heavy doors, and their small windows were situated higher than a man's reach and barred. In one of the cells, he had Jonathan put down a palette of straw for a bed.

Lady Debarlow opened her eyes when the carriage drew to a stop at the front doors of the manor, indicating to Montague that she had not indeed been sleeping. She looked out the window, but the morning light was still two hours away. He assisted the Baroness from the carriage and undid the bindings from her wrists. She looked up at him with a quizzical eye as she rubbed her wrists.

"You will find naught but hills and trees for miles," he told her as he took her by the elbow.

No one greeted them at the door for the servants had been dismissed years ago.

"And none save you, myself, and my valet as the occupants," he added in case she thought to seek the aid of someone else.

She turned to the driver, but he had turned the carriage around and was headed out the gates.

"My portmanteau?" she inquired. "Sir."

"Back at the posting inn with your abigail. We did not retrieve it as you will have no need for clothing here."

She halted in her steps but said nothing.

"Come," he urged, "your phantasy awaits."

He could tell she was tempted to snicker—a good sign for she would not have considered such a response if she did not feel somewhat at ease.

Jonathan opened the door for them and led them down a winding stairwell to the "dungeons." Montague had selected one of the brighter, more inviting cells. He instructed Jonathan to start a fire in the fireplace. Despite the warmer summer month, the chamber was still cool upon the skin. He could see from the frown upon Lady Debarlow that the accommodations did not excite her.

"The amenities will improve upon satisfactory performance," he informed. "We shall see how well *Madame Botreaux's* has prepared you. We begin tomorrow morning."

"I am to stay in this…cell?" she asked. "Sir?"

"Yes."

"But what if I should need to tend to myself, Sir?"

"Pardon?"

"Is there no one to assist me, Sir?"

"Jonathan will bring you a bell to ring should you require him."

"Him? Am I not to have an abigail?"

"Jonathan would be happy to service you. But you are to address him, too, as 'Sir.'"

The set of her jaw hardened but she lifted her chin slightly. "What if…what if I should need to relieve myself, Sir?"

"There is a chamber pot in the corner."

He thought she shuddered. Despite her humble origins, he doubted that she had had to suffer such demeaning conditions. The straw palette was a far cry from the silken sheets was accustomed to at present. From what her maidservant had told Jonathan, the Baroness was partial to the finer things in life. But her current meager surroundings were not intended to break her spirit. Any such attempts would be met by fierce resistance. Lady Debarlow would not be cowed. He felt stirred by her demeanor and found himself eagerly awaiting the morning.

"Have you any other questions, Baroness?"

She pressed her lips into a firm line. "None, Sir."

"Then I bid you good night."

He closed the door behind him. Once out of her view, he gratefully removed his mask and took a deep breath. His body buzzed with anticipation. He headed upstairs to the drawing room to find a bottle of drink to calm his nerves. He had never undertaken such an endeavor before. Then again, no one had ever commissioned him to seduce a woman before.

Penelope had taught him a great deal, but he could sense a significant amount of resistance in the Baroness. He had never before felt his confidence waver, but Lady Debarlow was no easy damsel to sweep off the feet. He would sooner deal with the frostiest of women. Indeed, he excelled at melting the icy armor that many women used to protect their hearts. Lady Debarlow was far from frigid. Quite the contrary, she exuded heat and passion. But she had her own set of armor.

The seduction of a woman involved more than an appeal to her lust, but with the Baroness, he would start with her body.

* * * * *

Abbey watched the valet start the fire and entertained for a moment the possibility of bludgeoning him over the head with an object and making her escape. But the chamber was barren, and even if she could slip past the man and find her way out of the place, she could not be certain where to go thereafter. They could be miles from the nearest person. But perhaps even the wilderness would prove a better prospect then her current prison?

The situation was outrageous. Not only was she a hostage thrown into some cell fit only for one's enemy, but she had to suffer the indignity of being serviced by a *man*. And to call him 'Sir' to boot! But if he thought her some dainty princess, he would discover her to be made of stronger mettle. Why she cared what her abductor thought of her struck her as odd. For all she knew, he might prove a madman.

"What is this extraordinary place?" she inquired of Jonathan, who might prove less aloof than his master.

"One that my lady has never been before till now," was the reply.

The valet intended to be as mysterious as his master, she deemed with disappointment. But she was not ready to give in completely.

"What part of England are we?"

"Why does my lady wish to know?"

"Does your master bring women here often?"

"On occasion."

"Does he treat them all with such 'hospitality?'"

The valet grinned. "You are a special captive, my lady."

"How am I to have been so fortunate?"

"My master is taken with you."

That gave her pause. The look of discomfort upon the valet, as if he realized he had disclosed too much, intrigued her.

"I am too old for flattery," she said, feigning disinterest. "What does he do with his female 'guests?'"

"It would depend upon the woman."

"And when he is done?"

He shrugged. "They depart."

"Of their own free will?"

"Aye."

The man appeared to speak truthfully, and she felt a small sense of relief. But she would not allow herself to be completely at ease.

"You have been in his employ long and have seen these women?"

"I have been in his service nigh on ten years."

Damn. He was likely quite loyal to his master, thought Abbey. But that did not mean he was entirely immune to persuasion. She looked him over. Like his master, he had a more athletic body with strong thighs, muscular calves, and square shoulders. He was younger—perhaps eight and twenty years of age—and, save for a slightly crooked nose, was quite attractive.

"A man like you could do much with twenty thousand pounds,"

she enticed. "You speak intelligently, have fine features. You need not be a valet all your life."

"Are you bribing me, my lady?"

"Surely there is something that you wish for?"

He turned to stoke the fire. "I am content in my situation."

She decided not to press the matter at the moment. Thus far he had obliged her, and she wanted him to continue answering her questions.

"Your master has not long been a patron of *The Cavern*. Was he a member elsewhere before?"

"I am not aware of it during my tenure with him, but it were quite possible he has not disclosed all to me."

"But you clearly have his trust for you are party to my capture. You realize I could have you brought to trial for this, and if convicted, you would be sent to Newgate. It be no small offense to kidnap a member of polite society."

"My master believes that you will not be pressing charges."

"Ha! And why is that?"

He looked at her candidly. "Because you will have enjoyed your stay here."

His response upset her with its implied arrogance. "If that were possible, why have I been assigned such poor accommodations?"

"I know not all that my master has planned for you. Suffice it to say that he is quite skilled in the art of pleasuring women."

She pursed her lips. Their conceit both vexed and intrigued her, but she did not want to display any anger before the valet. He may prove useful yet.

"Have you any water? I am feeling quite parched."

He bowed and left. To her disappointment, she heard a bolt slide into place. The door would be locked then. She took the opportunity to scan the rest of her surroundings. There would be no exit through the window, provided she could reach it. The only other exit beside the door would be the fireplace. The wooden door looked too heavy to be broken.

Jonathan returned with a canteen of water.

"Thank you," she said as she accepted the water. "I wonder that I have not come across your master before?"

She studied his face for a reaction. He blinked a bit rapidly and she suspected he was privy to intelligence.

"Or perhaps I have?" she ventured as she flashed through her mind the men that she knew at *The Cavern*—a futile exercise as she did not know the identity of all of them.

"Perhaps," he replied. "I know not all his acquaintances."

"I rather suspect you do."

He cleared his throat. "Is there anything else you require, Lady Debarlow?"

"My maid Jenny is no dolt. Upon discovering my absence, she will be quick to seek the authorities. We shall be found."

"I think, Lady Debarlow, by the time anyone should ascertain where you were taken, my master will be done with you."

He bowed and took his leave, but stopped upon the threshold. He strode back to her. She tensed, preparing to fend him off should he try to press his attentions upon her, though she doubted that his master would have given him permission to do so.

"I believe this to be yours?" He presented her glove. "I think you had dropped it upon the ground."

Frowning, she took the glove from him. He departed, leaving her in the dark and with the realization that no one was likely to rescue her.

CHAPTER THIRTEEN

MONTAGUE STARED DOWN at the woman lying upon the straw palette. Asleep, the Baroness appeared at peace and no longer *en garde*. He noted her lashes resting upon the curve of her cheek and the slight part of her lips. With her defenses down, she looked quite the innocent. Angelic. He had a strange desire to wrap her protectively in his arms. He hoped that she would not prove too resistant or obstinate to the program he intended for her as he would rather not force her to spend all her nights upon the straw bed.

His night spent upon the settee of the drawing room had not been considerably better. He could not in good conscience sleep upon a bed of feathers whilst she spent the night upon the floor. As a result, he had a crick in his neck despite having slept only three hours. Shortly after dawn, he had roused himself and downed a cup of coffee that Jonathan had brewed. After cleansing his body and receiving a shave, he felt much refreshed. He donned a pair of breeches, had his hair powdered, and replaced his mask. He was ready for the Baroness.

Her eyelashes flickered. She opened her eyes to find him standing above her.

"Good morning, Baroness," he greeted.

She quickly sat up. The blanket that he had had Jonathan place over her in the middle of the night fell from her shoulders. Her attire was rumpled and her hair disheveled, but she looked no less compelling.

He gestured to Jonathan, who stood behind him with a tray. "Will you partake of breakfast, Baroness?"

Her stomach grumbled in response. Jonathan set down before her the tray with a pot of coffee, stewed fruit, porridge, and eggs. She eyed the food keenly. He wondered if she was expecting water and stale bread.

"Eat well," he encouraged, "for you will require sustenance to bolster your endurance."

Requiring no further encouragement, she dove her fork into the eggs, bypassing any salt or pepper in her hunger. He watched as she then turned to the porridge. At one point she flicked her tongue over the corner of her mouth to catch a drop of milk. He felt his cock stir. He once knew a woman who used the consumption of strawberries as part of her seduction, but he had never thought to find porridge quite so alluring.

When the Baroness had finished her breakfast, having cleared everything including the last drop of coffee, she appeared much more content.

"What will you have me do, Sir?" she inquired. "Your submissive is eager to please."

He doubted the sincerity of her statement but at least she was making an attempt.

"You will undress yourself," he answered." Jonathan will assist in your toilette if you desire."

She inhaled sharply, clearly displeased, but she knew it was fruitless to object.

"Do you intend to watch, Sir?" she asked with raised brows.

"But of course," he answered somberly, though he wondered at the wisdom of doing so. The mere thought of her naked made his blood pound.

Grudgingly, she unbuttoned her *caraco*, but instead of lashes lowered modestly, she held his gaze as if daring him to look away. He knew some dominants trained their submissives to keep their heads lowered in deference, but he much preferred seeing the flash in her eyes and even enjoyed her defiance. She wrapped her finger and thumb about the last button and slowly pushed it through the button hole. She slid the jacket down her arms and allowed it to fall to the floor.

He swallowed hard. *Damnation.* And she had but removed one article of clothing.

Next she withdrew the pins from her skirts. With a quiet rustle, they crumpled to the ground. His cock had hardened when she stepped out of her petticoats. From the periphery of his eye, he saw that Jonathan was also unsettled.

"I will require assistance with my stays, Sir," she informed.

Jonathan stepped around her back—rather eagerly, Montague observed wryly. Unaccustomed to untying a woman's stays, Jonathan's large hands fumbled about for a while. He finally managed to unlace the ribbons. The Baroness stood in only her chemise, stockings, and garters. Montague admired her bare arms and the shape of her calves. He would have made quick work of what remained of her clothing, but he had never witnessed so enjoyable a demonstration as the undressing of Lady Debarlow.

"Am I sufficiently undressed, Sir?" she inquired.

"Not at all," he replied. "You are to strip to the buff."

Again her mouth turned down in displeasure, but she made no protest. She undid her garters first, then rolled down her stockings. There were few things lovelier than the shape of a woman's leg, Montague observed and recalled how he had massaged her feet. His hands wanted to caress what he saw. His desire lengthened against him. When she bared her shoulders, he groaned inwardly. He saw that he would have to constantly stiffen his resolve when it came to her. She saw the effect she was having upon and languidly slipped the chemise down past her breasts.

Dear bodkins. The two orbs accented with large rosy areolas stared at him in all their glory. They were magnificent. The perfect shape for her body. The perfect ripeness. Full and sufficiently heavy. They did not slump but protruded from her chest proudly.

The thin material dropped past her belly button, revealing another favorite part of the woman's body for him. The curves about the hips. The subtle swell of the abdomen and the flare of the hips were distinctive of the female sex—at least those who had passed puberty.

The final revelation would be her thighs and mons. Montague felt as if he had feasted upon more courses than he dared hope, and here was a second course of dessert set before him.

Her chemise joined the other articles of clothing about her feet. The Baroness stood before him completely naked. He could hardly believe his eyes. She had offered no resistance. He drank in the beauty before him, noting that Jonathan stood rooted to his spot.

"Are you pleased, Sir?" she asked brazenly.

He stared at the suppleness of her thighs. "Quite pleased, Baroness."

He walked around her and surveyed her gloriously naked body. She had the curves of a grown woman but the firmness of a woman who had not yet born children. Her arse was a particular delight. He had suspected it might be despite the layers of petticoats that had disguised her form. After staring at her backside in the carriage, he had speculated as to how her rump might strike him, and he was not disappointed. His hand longed to caress the arch of her arse, but he refrained. There would be opportunity enough in due time. Although the Baroness had complied with his orders, somehow she had acquired some of the balance of power in her undressing. He intended to shift authority back to him. He fixed his gaze at the patch of curls atop her mons, the blood in his veins throbbing at the delicious sight, and gestured to Jonathan.

The valet stepped outside and returned with a large bowl of water, razor, and cream. Abbey glanced at the items, then the two men, both of whom were clean shaven. She looked over her abductor and the smooth planes of his pectoral. She had been convinced that he was a gentleman, and yet the muscles about his abdomen were more like those of the laboring class. His body reminded her of a Grecian Olympian. She rather hoped that he would continue to be in a state of half-dress during the duration—especially if she herself were to be naked.

To be on such display, exposed before two complete strangers, engendered the most awkward sensations: a mingling of indignation, embarrassment, distress, and excitement. She attempted a nonchalance that belied her true agitation. Having been naked before at *Madame*

Botreaux's, she possessed more confidence in her nudity than most women might, but she had never been an exhibition, her most intimate parts bared for others to gape at. She was tempted to cover herself with her hands *a la* a chastened Eve. The air felt cool upon her skin despite the fire in the fireplace. She wondered what strange inclination her abductor had in making her watch one of them undergo a shave.

As if reading her mind, he informed her that the shaving accoutrements were for her benefit.

"Mine, Sir?" she echoed, balking at the thought of becoming bald. Did he truly intend to take all her hair? What sort of man became titillated by baldness?

"A mere trim," he said.

She followed his gaze to her mons. Although relieved that he did not mean the hair upon her head, the thought of a stranger touching a blade to her nether parts was nonetheless unsettling.

"Must we...?"

"Aye," he answered, crossing his arms.

Jonathan set the articles before her and went down upon one knee. His face was mere centimeters from her most private area. Her pulse quickened.

"I can shave myself, Sir," she stated.

He shook his head. "You will keep your arms behind you."

Her breath became uneven.

"Behind you," he reiterated.

Concluding that there was little she could do to dissuade him, she complied. Jonathan took a cloth and wiped the area above her thighs, then applied the shaving cream to her body. She closed her eyes at the coldness of the cream.

"Spread your legs."

Her eyes opened. Why should he require--?

"Now," he commanded grimly.

With a hard swallow, she shifted her feet apart. Jonathan brushed the cream over her labia. Next he took up the razor and gently scraped the blade along her lower pelvis.

"Worry not," he said, no doubt seeing that she held her breath. "Jonathan is quite skilled with the blade."

Save for the scratching of the razor, the chamber was silent for a moment. Montague could see her unease, which, when she looked into his eyes, manifested itself as anger. But he was not daunted, having seduced many a woman who first reviled him.

"You will wish to lie down," he informed her when Jonathan had finished the front.

Her eyelids fluttered but she obeyed. She lay down upon the cold stone ground and spread her legs. She gasped when Jonathan pressed a finger to her labia to stretch the flesh and create a more even plane for the blade, but she remained admirably in her position. Jonathan shaved the stray hairs curling over her quim, then sheared the length of the remaining patch of hair. He washed away the remnants of the cream before collecting everything and stepping away.

Montague went to inspect Jonathan's work. The pink flesh between her legs glistened from the moisture. He put a hand to her mons and felt the slickness of newly shaved skin. She flinched but made no protest. He slid a finger along the flesh below. Jonathan had done a splendid job cleaning the area, leaving a nice trim triangle of hair at the apex of her thighs.

"Feel how smooth you now are," he instructed.

She lifted her hand and felt her own silkiness. She felt the shorter hairs. It was not a disagreeable sensation. Provocative even? Her gaze found his. She saw the intensity of his eyes through his mask. He was familiar to her. She knew him—or had at least encountered him before. He held out his hand and assisted her to her feet.

"Now we may begin your training, Baroness."

He led her out and into the adjoining chamber. She was greeted by a number of apparatuses that she recognized from *The Cavern*. Some she had experienced, to great enjoyment.

"We shall make use of all of them," he assured her as he positioned her between two vertical poles of wood. A horizontal bar rested upon the two poles. She saw that the height of the bar could be adjusted. It currently rested at the highest point above her head.

Jonathan wrapped a rope about her left wrist and tied it to the far left end of the bar. He did the same to her other wrist to the other side of the bar, stretching her arms wide. Her ankles were tied to the bottoms of the poles so that her body formed an "X." She knew from watching the valet entwine the ropes that she was bound securely. The anticipation, roused already by the shave, grew exponentially. She looked at her master. He had a visible bulge between his legs—as did the valet. She knew that oftentimes that the true place of power rested with the submissive. If she pleased him enough, she might be able to exert some influence over him.

He appraised her in her new position. Satisfied, he strode over to her.

"Are you ready, my lovely Baroness?"

"Yes."

He raised his brows.

"Yes, Sir."

He shook his head a little sadly and slapped a breast. She cried out in surprise at the sudden strike.

"Come, come, Lady Debarlow. You are no novice."

"Forgive me, Sir," she ground out.

He cupped her chin and tilted her face to his. "Such disdain and defiance. No matter. You will submit to me yet."

He dropped her chin and walked behind her. It distressed her to have him out of sight. Her whole body became alert to what he might do.

"There is the matter of the spanking that you received a reprieve from," he noted. "I think it time we administer it."

He patted her derriere, then gave it a resounding slap. His hand did not have the bite of the crop or the sting of the tails, but the force made her jump nonetheless.

"Thank me," he instructed.

"Thank you, Sir."

"Raise your arse for me."

She obeyed to the best of her ability given that she was stretched by her bindings. He whacked her other cheek.

"Thank you, Sir," she grunted.

"Much better."

He backhanded one buttock on his way to striking the other. She inhaled sharply.

"Thank you, Sir."

"Your arse quivers delightfully, Lady Debarlow. Raise yourself onto your toes."

His next smack sent her back onto the flat of her feet. Her body strained against her bindings.

"Thank you, Sir," she said after a momentary lapse.

"Back on your toes."

Being on her toes made her back arch, pushing her derriere upwards. She wondered how many blows she would have to endure.

He rubbed the curve of her rump, then delivered a few more wallops that had her gasping. If the spankings were an indication of the force he intended to apply, she began to fear for what lay ahead.

"Baroness?"

"Thank you, Sir," she remembered.

"Tsk. Tsk. And I had thought you experienced in the role of the submissive."

"Forgive me. I am out of practice, as it were."

"We must teach your memory better."

He whacked her twice more on the same cheek. Her legs collapsed beneath her with the strength of the blows, her body held up by her bindings and the poles. She had not thought he could land a fiercer cuff.

"Thank you, Sir," she gasped after needing to take a conscious breath.

"Ask me if your arse is red enough."

"Is my arse red enough to please you, Sir?"

"It is the hue of a sunset, but I require the blush of a rose."

Her bottom felt hot from the spanking and she dreaded how it would feel when she sat down next, but she would not request leniency.

116

She was made of stronger mettle.

He rained a series of blows from differing directions. She attempted to thank him after every one.

"My favorite work of art, Baroness, would be the print of my hand upon your arse, I think."

"Thank you, Sir."

He grabbed a buttock and sank his fingers deep into the flesh. "Your arse, Lady Debarlow, belongs to me to do as I will. Do you understand?"

"Aye, Sir."

"Did your arse enjoy my attentions?"

"Aye, Sir."

"Then you shall beg for a spanking whenever you err."

"Aye, Sir."

He slipped his hand between her legs and stroked her quim—a touch so gentle compared to what she had sustained just prior that she inadvertently moaned. He softly brushed his fingers over her nether lips, then inserted a forefinger into her quim. She clenched her muscles about the uncomfortable intrusion, but when he withdrew, she was aware that she was a bit moist there. The heat from her buttocks had warmed the rest of her body.

"Jonathan, the salve."

The valet approached her and applied an oily substance to her derriere. At first, it felt like ice applied to fire but then settled into a relieving warmth. He spread it past her rump, down her legs, coating the entire limb. Next he applied the salve to her arms and back. Finally he attended the treatment to her chest, her breasts, her stomach, and loins until every inch of her body was buttered by the balm.

"And now," her abductor said, "the cat o'nine tails."

CHAPTER FOURTEEN

H ER BODY GLEAMED with the salve, which would offer her skin an amount of protection from the welts produced by the whip. Montague felt a stab of jealousy, having liked to apply the salve himself to the Baroness, but it had been scintillating in a different form watching Jonathan. His valet handed him the whip with its nine leather belts. He took the instrument and slapped it into the palm of his other hand.

"What do you like best about the tails, Baroness?" he inquired.

"Its breadth, Sir. The strike covers a larger area."

"Do you favor it over the crop?"

"I do, Sir."

"Do you revere it?"

"Aye, Sir."

He stepped up to her.

"Kiss it for me."

He held the whip to her lips. She pressed her mouth to it, then looked expectantly at him. He detected a touch of fear still in her eyes and decided upon a different approach before applying the nine-tails.

"Close your eyes," he directed softly.

Her eyes fluttered but she did as he bid.

"Recall the most exquisite touch upon your body. How it felt upon your body. Was it the tails kissing your skin?"

"No, Sir."

"The crop?"

"A man's hand, Sir."

"Where did he touch?"

"My cunnie, Sir."

He pushed away the rising jealousy he felt and continued. "Did he bring you to climax?"

"Aye, Sir."

"Imagine what else you would have him do to your body."

He observed the flare of her nostrils.

"What acts of lust would you engage with him? Would you venture into the wicked and depraved?"

She purred. He slipped the tails between her thighs and brushed it against her clitoris.

"Do you enjoy spending, Baroness?"

"Who does not?"

He moved the whip back and forth against her.

"Would you wish to spend over and over?"

"Indeed, Sir."

"You will spend—often—here if I am pleased with your performance. Your deepest, darkest desires will find their fulfillment here."

He removed the whip and saw with satisfaction that it glistened with her wetness. Now she was ready.

"First you must earn the right to spend," he informed her.

He stepped back and landed the lash across her side. She grunted. He laid it across her thigh. The straps glided over her slick skin.

"Thank you, Sir."

He rewarded her with a blow to her breasts. She cried out as one of the belts struck her across the nipple. He put the whip to her other breast. She strained against her bindings. Over and over he showered her body with the tails. A person witnessing the spectacle and hearing her cries might conclude it was pure torture. But when he cupped her quim, he found her even more wet. He circled his thumb over her clitoris. She shivered.

"Do you believe you deserve to spend?" he inquired.

"Yes, Sir."

"Then beg for it."

"Please, Sir, allow me to spend."

"I said *beg*, not state."

She groaned. "I beg of you, Sir, allow me to spend. I would be most grateful."

He flicked at her clitoris with his forefinger.

"What would you do to earn such an opportunity?"

"Anything you wish, Sir."

He agitated the nub of flesh with quicker ministrations. Her eyes rolled towards the back of her head and she moaned.

"Anything?"

"What do you please, Sir?"

He removed his hand, and it was as if the air was taken from her. She looked at him in astonishment.

"It would not be proper for the submissive to come before her masters, would it?"

Realizing the truth of what he said, she hung her head briefly. "It would not, Sir."

"I think my valet must need relief."

She sucked in her breath and glanced at Jonathan.

"I shall release your bonds, and you will apply yourself to him."

He untied her wrists and ankles, then pushed her down to her knees. *God help him.* He had never invited Jonathan into his liaisons before, but this was no ordinary situation.

"Take him into your mouth," he instructed.

Jonathan eagerly unbuttoned his breeches. His cock sprang out without ceremony. Lady Debarlow regarded his length. She did not appear repulsed by it. Without word, she took his length between her supple lips.

Montague nearly let out an oath. Oddly the feelings of jealousy fueled his arousal. The blood rushed to his groin. He looked to his valet. The man had better be loyal unto death after this.

The Baroness moved her mouth up and down Jonathan's shaft with a comfort that indicated she was no neophyte when it came to fellatio. Jonathan grabbed the back of her head and pushed her further onto his cock. She gagged a little but relaxed and was able to accommodate his length. Fisting his hand in her hair, Jonathan bucked his hips at her face. With each thrust, Montague felt his own cock tightening.

"Pleasure yourself," he ordered her, "but do not spend till you have been granted permission to do so."

She reached a hand between her legs and fondled herself. Montague stroked the swell at his crotch. *What a magnificent woman.* To take the cock of a man while tending to herself.

Jonathan grunted, then became red in the face. Body twitching, he let out a howl as he bucked his climax into her mouth. Montague watched her swallow the seed of his valet. Jonathan stumbled backwards, his cock pulling out of her mouth. Drops of his seed fell from the corner of her lips. She coughed a little but recovered quickly.

"Surely that merits a reward, Sir?" she asserted. "I would wager a common strumpet could not have done much better."

"It were an impressive performance," Montague conceded.

"I wish to spend then, Sir."

"Not quite yet."

Her brows rose. "Was that not pleasurable, Sir? How many can claim to witness a woman of title performing fellatio upon a *servant*."

"There is more, Baroness."

Her eyes flashed. "I have never before degraded myself in such a manner."

"Never? That would be disappointing given your reputation."

She pressed her lips together tightly. He had spoken too hastily.

"What know you of my reputation, Sir?"

"I know your family to be of bourgeois origins, but do not misunderstand me. I render no judgment. That you landed yourself a Baron is quite commendable."

"You think I made myself a whore to gain his hand in matrimony."

"A man such as the Baron Debarlow has access to whores enough without having to marry one, but given your station, I doubt the marriage to have been an agreement to solidify fiduciary interests. And I am not such a romantic to believe that the two of you had fallen in love."

"Because you do not believe in love, Sir?"

"I believe it exists, but it is a rare species, especially in matrimony. Do you profess that you loved the Baron or he you?"

"I am less a romantic than you," she returned, surprised at their topic of discussion and that she had an interest in speaking with him about it. "What I had with the Baron might approximate love, but Love between a man and a woman, in its truest form, is but a flight of fancy. It does not exist."

"You have never been in love? Even as a young woman?"

"I have *lusted* after men. Baron Debarlow was a friend and a lover. But no, I have never felt that which might be dubbed Love."

Her response, as well as her dispassionate tone, stunned and impressed him. Most of the women he knew harbored some sentimentality when it came to Love. They may have disdained Love, quite often because they had had their hearts broken at Her hand, but none had denied its very existence. He believed her when she said that Debarlow was a friend. The Debarlow maidservants had told Jonathan that they observed affection between the two. Perhaps the Baron had been in love with her.

"You are an extraordinary woman, Lady Debarlow," he thought aloud.

Her expression softened at his surprising statement.

"But I will not grant you permission to spend—yet."

Recalling her earlier anger, she blurted, "Why? Sir."

"It will prove more powerful after a period of forestalling. I know you to be quite aware of this as you have employed the art of deprivation on others."

"Have you been sent to avenge my actions? Sir."

"I recommend a less combative posture, Baroness, if you are to enjoy your time here. But if you will persist in being at loggerheads with me, I fear you will not avail yourself of the bounty of pleasure that awaits you."

She lowered her lashes and considered the merit of his statement.

"I will do as you say, Sir," she said when she looked up.

"Much better."

He looked over at Jonathan, who had recovered and stood at attention for the next command. He walked over to a large wooden board fixed at an incline.

"Mount her upon it," he instructed Jonathan.

The Baroness had her wrists tied above head and secured to the iron ring attached to the plank. Her legs were bent at the knee and tied apart, exposing her quim. Montague walked up to her. Her cunnie was at the perfect height for his cock. He rubbed his thumb along the length of her clitoris. She moaned her pleasure. He took some of the salve into his hand and rubbed it upon her, then quickened his motions. She squealed in delight. He sank a finger into the warm, wet folds of her womanhood. The sound of her grunting and groaning renewed his ardor. It took all of him not to tear off his breeches and fuck her then and there.

Jonathan approached him with a bowl of clothespins. She saw them and took an audible breath, knowing what was to come. But Penelope had told him that a woman could tolerate an exceptional level of pain, perhaps more so then men. Montague did not doubt the possibility as women had to be made strong enough for the pains of labor. And the Baroness was no weakling.

He pinched the side of her breast and affixed a pin.

"Thank you, Sir," she grunted.

He clipped more below the breast and had three in a row along her rib. He laced all the pins together with rope, then did the same on her other side. She took in her breaths carefully, her eyes moist with possible tears. Penelope had fastened such pins to him to provide him an appreciation of how it felt. He remembered how forcefully the pins had dug into his flesh. Stepping back, he examined his work. If he were a painter, he might seek to capture the vision of the Baroness bound and splayed before him, her sides decorated with the pins.

After giving the ends of the ropes to Jonathan, he returned to stroking the nub of flesh protruding impishly from her folds. He teased it until he had her panting and writhing.

"Please, Sir, may I spend?" she whispered.

"Before your master has spent himself?"

"How may I please you then, Sir?"

He glanced down at her cunnie and the rosy hole of her anus. The latter he would save for latter. He unbuttoned his breeches and freed his cock. The shaft sprang eagerly from its confines. His whole body was fit to burst if he did not attend to his erection.

She stared at the long thickness pointed at her. Licking her lips, she said, "Would you fuck me with your cock, Sir?"

He closed his eyes and groaned. His ears had never been graced with sweeter words. Positioning his cock near her quim, he rubbed it first along her folds to coat it with the salve. He slapped at her clitoris with his cock. She wiggled in her bindings and moaned. He rubbed himself more vigorously against her.

"Yes, yes," she encouraged.

Although her thighs were spread wide, it seemed she attempted to open her legs more to improve the area of exposure. When he sensed her agitated frenzy approaching a peak, he stepped away. He had not given her permission to spend.

"Please," she gasped. "Please *fuck me, Sir.*"

Montague attempted to calm the rapid beating of his heart. How glorious that she enjoyed her own body and had no reservations asking—nay, demanding—her desires. Her boldness heated an already scalding desire pounding within him.

As if their roles were reversed and she had become the mistress, she stared him in the eyes and said, "Sink your cock into my cunnie, Sir. I wish to feel you hard and thick inside me."

How warm and airless these quarters felt! He could not restrain himself after hearing such words or he would die of suffocation. He pushed his cock into her cunnie. She cried out in gratification. Encased by her hot, wet womanhood, he could have shot his load within seconds. He remained motionless, taking in several breaths, as he forced back the wave of his climax. She wickedly flexed her muscles about his cock and squirmed. He gasped and dug his grip into the wooden board. He intended she should climax before him, and spending quickly would cede the balance of power to her. Gritting his teeth, he envisioned the Earl of Frotham and the loss of Chelton. Twenty thousand pounds was at stake, he reminded himself. As well as his manhood.

When he had regained control, he slowly slid his cock back. Holding onto the wooden board behind her, his chest a hair's length from her breasts, he returned her stare. Time for a little set down. He pushed his cock into her.

"Ohhh…" she moaned.

He slid out until only the head remained inside of her, then slammed into her, burying himself deep inside her cunnie. She cried out in surprise. He thrust more deliberately, ensuring that he rubbed along her clitoris with every motion. She groaned her delight. Constrained by the bindings, she had little mobility in her hips, but there was little she could do under the force of his movements and was content to receive his assaults. The sound of flesh slapping against flesh filled the chamber, interspersed with her cries.

He grunted a reminder in her ear. "Not yet, Baroness."

She gave a despairing moan. Remembering how cool she had been to him at the park, he inserted his hand between them and fondled her clitoris. She gasped and thrashed against her bonds. He fell into a rhythm that had her straining and grinding her teeth. She dug her fingers into her palms in her attempt to stave off her climax.

"Please, Sir," she gasped hoarsely.

"No," he replied sternly.

Perspiration dotted her forehead. She made all manner of sounds and writhed with such intensity that the ropes about her wrists were sure to chafe her skin. He could not wager as to who would be more successful in holding back their climax. Her cunnie felt far too wonderful. The sweat trickled down from his temple as he held back his release. Now she struggled to get away from him as he continued to buck himself between her legs. Her grunts became increasingly guttural, and he sensed her peak nearing. He shortened his strokes and pounded into her at a rapid pace to push her over the edge.

A slow wail tore from her throat. Her body convulsed. Jonathan yanked the pins off her body. Her scream pierced the air. He felt her spasming about his cock. Pulling out of her, he allowed himself his long desired release, spilling his seed upon her leg. He shuddered and turned around so that he could throw back his mask to drink in much needed air. He unclenched the muscles that he had been tensing. Replacing his mask, he turned back to look at her. Her chest heaved heavily from the exertion. Her eyes were closed, and her head rested upon her arm.

He was glad that she had spent. He wanted fulfillment for her. But now he would have to punish her.

CHAPTER FIFTEEN

BBEY FELT AS IF HER body had been thrown into another world. He had built wave upon wave of ecstasy in her, and it took all of her to contain the flood for as long as she did. The explosiveness of her release, combined with the excruciating flash of pain when the pins were pulled from her body, created the most intense sensation her body had ever experienced. Her heart still hammered madly between the walls of her chest, and she wondered if it would ever return to normal.

When the world had finally righted itself and she felt some semblance of her senses had returned—as well as the soreness of her limbs—she slowly pried her eyes open to find him staring at her. She immediately knew what was to come.

"Spending without permission may be deemed an error. Spending before your master has done is a grave offense," he informed her.

"Forgive me, Sir," she mumbled, though she only half-regretted her transgression. She was too exhausted to care overmuch.

"You will be given a reprieve that you may have the strength to fully appreciate the punishment awaiting you."

Jonathan released her binds and caught her as she slumped towards the floor. He carried her to the corner and lowered her into a cage that had perhaps been meant for some predatory animal such as a tiger. Her heart sank at her new quarters.

"You see that you have a pan of water to drink from and a pan to piss in," she was told.

"How long am I to stay here, Sir?" she asked.

"As long as I deem necessary."

Of course. How silly of her to think that he would provide a candid answer. She attempted to find a comfortable position.

"Rest well," he bid her before departing with the valet.

Left alone, Abbey lay upon her side with her legs bent at the knee for the cage was not long enough for her to stretch her full length. She stared at the side of the cage in disbelief. A mixture of fear and excitement persisted. She had not thought she could spend in such a fashion. She had not expected to be aroused by him. But he had quite the arsenal of methods. And his touch...

She had to wonder if she had lain with him before for he seemed to know her body, knew how and where to fondle her. She considered all her past lovers but could not discern any of them to be her abductor. Only one man who had caressed her but with whom she was less familiar remained a possibility.

Montague Edwards.

It was plain her abductor disguised his voice, but he did have the same height as Edwards. Not having seen Edwards naked, she could not tell if his body was as sculpted in the same manner. But he had a similar leg. She recalled the fingers and how they had plied her clitoris. The memory of it renewed the warmth in her loins. Her thoughts still felt scrambled, but there was no denying her body responded to him—her abductor and Montague Edwards. Even now, after having had the most dramatic *orgasm*, she yearned for his touch.

Her hand crept between her legs and she languidly toyed with her clitoris. The spanking had been well done. The flogging exceptional. He was a practiced dominant. He had awakened nearly every part of her body. Even the more shameful parts—being forced to undress before the two men, having taking the cock of his valet into her mouth, and pleasuring herself before him—aroused a wicked desire within her. She liked the way her fingers slid against her flesh, made slippery by the salve.

If her abductor should be Montague Edwards, why would he wish to kidnap her? Was it merely to revel in carnal lust? She stroked herself more quickly at the thought that a man might be so wicked as to have that as his sole purpose. But how brazen of him to think that she would respond.

And respond she did, she thought ruefully. While desiring more. If he could elicit such breathtaking sensations from her body when she had not pleased him, what manner of pleasure could he evoke after she did please him? Her body shivered at the thought. She could feel her desire building despite her enervation. She flicked at her clitoris with vigor. The resulting climax relieved her agitation but did not prove nearly as satisfying as it once did.

She felt tired but restless and eager for his return. An hour or two passed. She drank of the water and eyed the other pan with dread. Prior to being a patron of *Madame Botreaux,* she would have been mortified, and although she felt a stab of humiliation, she knew that ultimately the punishment being wielded, if he were a proper dom, were for her benefit as much as his. Pushing aside her pride, she relieved herself into the pan.

Jonathan returned at one point to retrieve the sullied pan and provide water and bread.

"How long does your master intend to keep me locked in here?" she inquired.

"Sir," he reminded her.

"Sir."

"I know not, my lady."

His address struck her as odd given that she was caged like an unruly pet. Jonathan left and she shifted about uncomfortably for another hour. At last her abductor returned. She eyed him through the cage, but with his mask, she was unable to discern his identity with confidence. He opened the top of the cage and held out his hand to lift her out. She stepped out, grateful to be able to stretch her cramped limbs. Seeing that he held her crop, she was confident that the man had visited, if not frequented, *The Cavern.*

He pulled a chair from the corner and sat in it, pulling her on top of him and setting aside the crop. She could feel his hardened desire against her arse, but he still had on his breeches. He rubbed her sore arms with firm thorough motions, relaxing the muscles that had strained against the ropes. Tenderly he massaged her neck, melting away the tension. Suddenly she recognized the touch. It was the same caress she had received in the East Library of the Bennington ball.

It was Montague Edwards!

Her heart palpitated briskly at the knowledge. Relief, that her abductor was not some strange madman but a man she knew, waved over her. Agitation followed. She had been glib with him at St. James' Park. Was this his way of returning her dismissal? Yet a part of her thrilled that she had merited such *elaborate* attention from him. And she had thought he had no interest in her…

But how naughty of him to have made her take the cock of his valet into her mouth! And how skilled he was with the flogger. He was a man of many talents. She flushed to think that he had discovered her to be a patron of *Madame Botreaux*. She felt no shame in her patronage, of course, but found it unsettling that he had known of her identity without her prompting it.

He reached through her arms and cupped her breasts, scattering her thoughts. He kneaded the heavy flesh and brushed his thumbs over her nipples, which hardened instantly. She felt a familiar warmth building between her legs.

Should she reveal that she knew his identity? No, she should save it for a more opportune time, when she could think more properly, when his hand was not sliding down towards her mons. His fingers slid through the hair there until they found her clitoris once more. A few strokes and she felt her wetness pooling upon his thighs. She could no longer hide the fact that he had mastery over her body. He plunged two fingers into her cunnie. She arched her back into his hand. How she wished it were his cock pushing in and out of her!

As he fondled a breast with one hand, he continued to stir the most rousing and exquisite sensations in her nether parts. She hoped that he would allow her to spend this time.

But it was not to be.

He withdrew his hands, pushed her to her feet, and retrieved the crop.

"Kneel there," he commanded, pointing to a mattress against the wall.

She did as told. He bent her over by pushing her head to the bed. She turned her head to the side to breathe.

"Reach for your ankles."

He tied her wrists to her ankles. He stood behind her and gently caressed her derriere, arched in the air by her position.

"How fares my arse?"

"Well, Sir."

"Did you rest well in your cage?"

"As well as possible, Sir."

"Did you sleep?"

"No, Sir."

"Did you partake of the water?'

"I did, Sir."

"Did you take a piss?"

Her cheeks colored. "Aye, Sir."

"How else did you pass the time?"

"By being grateful for what you have given me, Sir."

"An acceptable fib. Did you engage in any other activity?"

She considered how she had pleasured herself but had not been given permission to do so.

"No, Sir."

The crop landed sharply on the bottom of her foot. She gasped at how much the strike smarted.

"How else did you occupy your time, Baroness?"

"I—I recalled the day, Sir."

"And?"

"That is all, Sir.:"

Whack! He struck the bottom of her other foot.

"Do you think me a simpleton that I cannot detect your lies? Jonathan told me that he saw you pleasuring yourself. Had I given you permission to touch yourself?"

"No, Sir."

He landed the crop against her arse.

"Did you spend?"

"Aye, Sir," she mumbled.

He whipped her again.

"Had I given you permission to spend?"

"No, Sir."

Reaching beneath her, he pinched a nipple and twisted it until she cried.

"Forgive me, Sir, forgive me."

He sighed. "One would think you wished to be punished, Baroness."

"No! I wish to please you. Pray, give me another chance, Sir."

He spread the cheeks of her derriere. She felt the tip of the crop circling her anus.

"Have you taken a cock here before?"

"Aye, Sir."

"Often?"

"A number of times, Sir."

"Did you enjoy it?"

"Aye, Sir."

He dipped a finger into her cunnie juice and inserted the digit into her sphincter. She gasped at the initial discomfort. He sawed his finger in and out of her slowly until she adjusted to the intrusion. She felt something cool, smooth, and hard in her cunnie. A cock made of glass perhaps? Once coated with her wetness, he reinserted it into her anus. It was too large at first and she had to make a concerted effort to relax the muscles of her sphincter to accommodate the invasion. She felt as if her entire body were plugged.

"Thank you, Sir."

He slid the crop along her cunnie and clit. She moaned her appreciation. He rubbed more vigorously until her body hummed with delight, overpowering the discomfort of her full anus. She heard him shed his breeches. He knelt behind her. She cried out when she felt his cock sinking into her quim. It seemed her body could not tolerate another penetration, but she knew from past experience that it could. Indeed, to be filled to the hilt in both holes was nothing short of extraordinary. Edwards began thrusting into her cunnie. The discomfort in her anus had melded with the other sensations, creating a divine overload of her senses. She gritted her teeth, knowing she had not been given permission to spend.

"Shall I spend first this time?" he inquired as he pummeled into her at a steady and even pace.

"Of course, Sir."

Driving his cock deeper inside of her, he bucked forcefully into her. She felt him shake against her and heard him groan. His hot seed streamed once more upon her leg. She half wondered that he did not spend inside of her but was more concerned with seeking her own relief.

"May I spend, Sir?"

He slipped his hand between her thighs and rubbed her.

"You should like to, would you not?"

Was he daft?

"Very much, Sir."

He played with her clitoris until she was dizzy with delight.

"But you have yet to pay for your past transgressions."

Damnation.

He removed the object from her derriere, and stepping away from her, retrieved an object made of iron.

"For pleasuring yourself until climax, we will have to make use of an age-old contraption," he explained. "A chastity belt."

She frowned but feared objection would only bring greater castigation. She knew that she had behaved poorly and must now pay the price.

He fixed the heavy belt about her, then released the ropes about her ankle and wrists. He pulled her to her feet.

"I will grant you one reprieve, however."

She looked at him hopefully. Her body was in an unbearable state of arousal.

"You need not spend the night in the cage."

He picked up his breeches and left. As soon as he was gone, she began tampering with the lock of the chastity belt. She would risk being punished again, but, by God, she needed to spend. The lock remained secure to her dismay. She pulled at the belt and attempted to grind her quim against it, but it was of no use. She collapsed back onto the bed. Perhaps she could cool her ardor with unsavory thoughts. Thoughts such as…

But her mind wandered back to the sound fucking she had just received. A fucking that had not ended to her fulfillment. Her hands cupped her breasts where he had held her moments before. She kneaded her breasts as he had done. Perhaps she could climax without direct stimulation of her clitoris or cunnie? She pulled at her nipples and circled her hips. She considered calling out his name, but what if he should be alarmed that she knew his identity and did not return?

She howled in frustration as she tossed and squirmed about the mattress, her body tense with a distress that need calming, a heat that needed extinguishing. She knew not how she managed to doze in her condition, but she drifted in and out of sleep, waking to the same agitation. Half-dreams and memories flitted through her mind: of her and Edwards in the library, of her taking his cock into her mouth, of her spending upon his hand. She dreamed of herself suspended in space in the center of the *Cavern* assembly floor. Edwards, wearing his mask, sauntered around her, demonstrating before a crowd of *Madame Botreaux's* patrons how he controlled her body. She responded to his every touch without feeling the slightest shame or discomfiture.

When she opened her eyes, morning had entered the chambers. Jonathan brought coffee and a bowl of porridge. He undid her chastity belt that she might make use of the chamber pot. She considered notifying the valet of her newfound knowledge, but he might warn his master. Curious to see what else Edwards had in store for her, she decided to save her trump card.

CHAPTER SIXTEEN

JONATHAN HAD TIED THE Baroness back onto the large wooden board and covered her eyes with a kerchief. With her vision denied, Montague was free to discard his mask and powder. The mere sight of her naked body generated a fever in him, and the mask was damnably warm. Walking into the chamber, his cock stiffened instantly upon seeing Lady Debarlow bound and exposed once more. He hoped that she would prove more obedient that he could grant her permission to spend. It was a lovely thing to see a woman in the throes of ecstasy.

"Good morning, Baroness," he greeted. "I pray that you had a peaceful night."

"You speak with irony, Sir," she accused.

"I own the thought of you struggling to satiate your arousal is titillating. Are you not now more eager to spend?"

"I should be most grateful to spend, Sir."

Stepping towards her, he ran the end of the flogger between her breasts. "Then let us begin."

He unfurled the tails and lashed it across her body.

She gasped. "Thank you, Sir."

He laid the straps between her thighs. She cried out and trembled. "Thank you, Sir."

He rewarded her appreciation with a stroke of the rosebud at her quim. She groaned. He stepped back and aimed the whip at her breast.

She ground her teeth together. "Thank you, Sir."

He put the whip to her other breast. She screamed when one of the belts struck her square on the nipple. He applied the tails to her inner thigh, then once more upon her cunnie. Moisture glistened upon her folds. He touched his finger to her wetness and then to her mouth. She closed her lips about his finger and sucked the juices of her own desire.

"Jonathan, the nipple clamps," he requested.

Her nipples were already deliciously erect and looked absolutely mouthwatering adorned by the clamps. He tugged lightly at the chain connecting the two nipple clamps.

"Thank you, Sir," she said between difficult breaths.

"Apply the weights."

She groaned an oath.

"Pardon?"

She bit her lower lip, then replied, "In truth, I abhor the weights upon my nipples, Sir."

"Your honesty is appreciated." He turned to Jonathan. "Apply the weights."

She threw her head back against the board in resignation. As Jonathan affixed the weights, Montague stroked her clitoris. At first she grunted from the pain of the load upon her nipples, but as he fondled her more vigorously, she squirmed in delight. He replaced his fingers with the whip and rubbed the honey from her cunnie about her nether lips. The scent of her arousal drifted into his nostrils, heating his blood. Desperately he wanted to feel her about his cock once more, but he wanted to wrest from her body climax after climax. He rubbed her between the legs until, trembling, she begged to spend.

"You may," he granted and watched with satisfaction as her body jerked against the restraints, her pelvis thrusting against him.

A shudder went through her before she relaxed with a relieved sigh. The flush in her cheeks was pure beauty, one that rouge could not replicate. Invigorated, he could spend the entire day pleasuring her.

"Release her from her bonds," he instructed Jonathan, "and stand her up."

He bound her wrists together behind her back, then wrapped a rope above her breasts, around her arms, and under her breasts, capturing the two orbs between the cords. His valet had been most compliant, and Montague decided to reward Jonathan for his service.

"Take her over the chair."

Jonathan pulled the chair over, bent the Baroness over the back of it, and shed his breeches. Montague watched with mixed feelings as the other man's cock disappeared into her. Holding onto her waist, Jonathan pounded into her cunnie.

"May I also pleasure you, Sir?" she asked.

"In due time," he replied though his body roared at him to accept the temptation. "First, you will spend once more for me."

She readily obliged, groaning with each stab. Closing her eyes, she moved in concert to Jonathan. Praising the heavens, Jonathan shoved himself deep into her. A paroxysm raked his body as he bucked against her rump, then staggered backwards as his seed shot from his cock. He rubbed his own length to coax the last of the cum, shuddered, and looked to Montague with appreciation.

"Place her on the bed, then leave us," Montague instructed his valet.

That would be the last time he allowed Jonathan to fuck Lady Debarlow. The Baroness would be his and his alone from now on.

He parted her thighs and stared at the wetness shining upon her quim.

"We are quite the wanton, Baroness," he noted.

"As are you, Sir," she returned.

He slid a finger along her folds. She shivered.

"I freely admit my depravity," he acknowledged as he positioned himself between her legs, "but you, Baroness, have inspired me to new heights."

"You flatter me, Sir."

Lowering himself, he inhaled her sweet musk and licked her folds.

"Have you done with punishing me, Sir?"

"Why do you ask?"

He flicked at her clitoris, making her gasp.

"I hesitate to relinquish myself if you are to forbid me to spend,

Sir."

He smiled at her. "You cannot prevent your body from reacting to my caresses, my dear."

To prove his point, he tongued the length of her womanhood. She moaned. Applying himself fervently, he elicited a chorus of groans, gasps, whimpers, and cries. Her toes curled. Her back arched. Her climax exploded in shudders throughout her body. She coiled and thrashed. He slowed his tongue until her tremors dissipated.

"Thank you, Sir," she murmured.

He wanted to begin anew and see her spend once again. Sitting up, he circled his thumb about her clitoris. It was as if he could not desist from touching her. She lay quietly as if in slumber. Rising to his feet, he resisted the ache in his loins and the fire in his blood and went in search of Jonathan.

* * * * *

Abbey heard Edwards leave but was halfway asleep. Jonathan returned to undo the ropes about her and to remove her blindfold. He held out a robe for her.

"Come," he said.

Slipping on the silk robe, she followed him, surprised when he led her out of the chambers and up a stairwell. What did Edwards have in store?

Jonathan led her to a second floor and into a bed chamber sumptuous in comparison to her previous quarters. In an anteroom, she saw that a bath was prepared for her. She dared to hope that it was meant for her. In addition to the various fluids upon her body, she was still covered with the slick salve that he had applied.

"Will you require assistance with your bath, my lady?" he asked.

The thought of solitude was inviting at the moment, so she shook her head. He poured a glass of wine for her and left it near the bath. With a bow, he left the room.

Taking the glass, she settled herself into the warm, soapy water. It had been scented with…orange blossom? The bath felt *divine*. It cradled her sore limbs. She was unsure that she wished to ever move from it. She sipped the burgundy. A fine wine, she mused as the flavor of berries and a hint of pepper cascaded over her tongue. Without doubt, Edwards seemed to know how to please and satisfy her—especially her carnal senses. Never had her body been so delightfully tormented. Never had she known such greed. Seconds after spending, she yearned for his touch more once more. She *wanted* to submit to him. He was everything that Tremayne was not.

Could she contemplate returning to Charles after this experience? The thought, not unlike the prospect of having to study Latin after a night of carousing and merrymaking, wearied her. Every touch of his would only remind her of Edwards. She would not be able to hide her resentment of Charles. Which only made it more imperative that she wed him as quickly as possible before her disdain for him became too obvious. Then she might return to Edwards, if he would consider being her paramour—a prospect much more inviting than Latin…

After finishing the wine and soaking until her skin pruned, she scrubbed herself with the sponge and washed her hair. Feeling refreshed, she would never take for granted a good bath. After drying herself, she ventured into the bedroom. It was an elegantly appointed room without being ornate. The curtains of the Palladian windows were pulled aside to allow in the warm glow of dusk. Tapestries hung from the walls and a large rug covered the floor. On the four post bed lay a fresh pair of stockings, petticoats, and chemise. A man's banyan hung from an armoire. She opted to wrap herself in the banyan. Beside the bed, supper had been spread upon a small table: meat pastries, beef, asparagus, potted cheese, sweetmeats candied orange peels, and a decanter of wine. Next to the supper was a small silver snuffbox. Abbey smiled, recalling their first encounter. She took a pinch of snuff before sitting down to partake in the meal.

"How does my lady find her supper?"

She looked up from her plate at Edwards, standing upon the threshold, masked and wearing a shirt this time with his breeches. His hair was powdered once more.

"Very well, Sir. Have you come to return me to my cell?"

"No. We have done with the dungeons. You will sleep here tonight."

"Why the superior treatment?"

"Because you have pleased me."

She thought a moment. "But you have not spent today, Sir."

"Your pleasure was enjoyment enough for me."

"You have an admirable forbearance, Sir."

He chuckled—a rare sound that warmed and thrilled her.

"I surprised myself," he admitted.

She took a bite of pastry. "What lies ahead for me, Sir?"

He fell silent.

"Home," he said at last.

Surprised, she echoed, "Home?"

"Yes. You will be returned home."

She could not help but be disappointed. "Have I displeased you, Sir?"

"On the contrary. I had stated that you pleased me. I would add 'immensely.'"

She should be pleased that she was being released, but she could not help asking, "Then why send me home?"

His voice seemed to crack a little. "Have you a wish to stay?"

Her heart pounded at the answer. She should return to London and marry Charles. That had been her aim. One that she had carefully planned that she might have the ultimate revenge upon the Earl of Frotham. Now she intended to risk that by extending her stay with Montague Edwards?

"I would own that my experience here rivals any that I have had at *Madame Botreaux's*," she replied.

He took a tempting step toward her, then retreated. "I am glad of it, Lady Debarlow."

She knit her brows. Was he done with her? Was this the common length of stay for most of his conquests?

"I have seen you before at Madame Botreaux's, Sir. Why did you not seek me then?"

"I was waiting for the proper opportunity. And I preferred to have you alone, away from prying eyes."

"Are you the proprietor here, Sir?"

"At present."

Why did he not answer simply in the affirmative? But she did not pursue the matter.

"From what I have seen, it is quite exceptional."

"It was once a Norse castle."

She heard the emotion in his voice. She wanted to know more about this place and about him, but that were not possible if she were sent home. But the longer she left Charles to his own, the more likely he was to be persuaded by his father.

"It appears quite the special place. Tell me more, Sir."

He hesitated but then proceeded to describe some of the history, at least what he was able to discern from years of research. As he spoke, she sensed his demeanor relaxing. It was clear he held the place with affectionate regard.

"Has this property been with your family long then?" she inquired.

"It would be three generations if..."

"If?"

"Your clothes have been washed. If they are dry, you can depart in the morning."

But she had no wish to leave. She decided she would take a chance and delay her return if she could.

"And if I wish to stay, Sir?"

"We are done, Baroness."

Pushing aside her dinner, she rose to her feet. "How might I persuade you to extend my stay, Sir?"

He crossed his arm. "You cannot."

"Indeed?"

She walked to him. Standing before him, she untied the sash of the banyan and let the robe fall from her shoulders.

CHAPTER SEVENTEEN

THE GLORY OF HER nakedness struck him with more force than sunbeam in darkness. Montague had to shut his eyes to gather himself. He had decided to conclude her stay at Chelton more for his sake than hers. She was proving too much a temptation. He wanted to fuck her all day and all night. His sense of control was slipping away. He needed time away from her, but the Caprice of Fate would not make his decision easy. That Lady Debarlow expressed a desire to stay ought to have been music to his ears. Indeed, he fair quivered at the thought of having her longer, of the many ways he could indulge her body. He shook away the thoughts. He had made his decision and ought not to waver.

"I would submit to your every desire, Sir," she offered.

He felt a growl in the back of his throat, but replied instead, "Your temperament does not befit a pure submissive."

"Are you not master enough, Sir?" she challenged.

With a silent curse, he suppressed the urge to grab her and show her the extent of his mastery.

"Such impudence will merit you a sound punishment."

"Then punish me, Sir."

The mischievous shimmer in her eyes had his cock at instant attention.

She took the distance between them and stood with her nipples nearly grazing his shirt. The blood churned in his groin. When she brushed against his erection with her thigh, he nearly lost his mind. Damn this woman. How could his body respond so eagerly to her? He was about to speak, but the words caught in his throat when she cupped his bulge with her hand.

Gathering his resolve, he removed her hand. "You will desist, Baroness."

But she defied him and sank to her knees. She eyed his crotch. With her other hand she sought his buttons.

"Cease!" he barked. If she were to touch his cock—or, God help him, take him into her mouth—all resolve would be lost.

She paid him no heed and licked at his cock through his breeches. Quickly, he pulled her away from him. Grabbing the banyan off the floor with his other hand, he dragged her towards the bed.

"Clothe yourself," he ordered as he deposited her on the bed and pushed the robe at her.

She frowned. "Are you afraid of what I might do, Sir?"

"If you wish to believe it."

"But why? You cannot deny that you are aroused." She gave a pointed glance at his crotch, then added tauntingly, "Sir."

"I am a man. As such, little provocation is required."

His response angered her. "But you have yet to experience the extent of my skills, Sir."

"The charade is over."

He turned to leave.

"Indeed," she declared. "For I know who you are. Montague Edwards."

He stopped at his name. How the devil did she know? Had she known all this time?

"You need not gone through such extravagance, Mr. Edwards. You could have approached me in *The Cavern*."

Jonathan would not have revealed him, he was convinced. He turned around with surprising calm despite the racing of his heart. He removed his mask—with relief.

"Your perception, Baroness, is quite impressive."

"Were it not more appropriate to address me by my given name? As you know me in the most intimate terms. Sir."

"You need not address me such. Montague will suffice."

She deliberated. "Montague."

He gave a low grunt, liking the sound of his name upon her lips.

"Why did you not approach me in *The Cavern*?" she asked.

"Would you have accepted my advances?" he returned. "You seem quite committed to the Viscount."

She acknowledged the truth of his statement with a nod.

"And it were far more exciting to abduct you," he added.

She smiled, the lust returning to her eyes. "Do you still wish me to leave, Sir?"

He groaned. *Hell and damnation.* The fact that she knew his identity and still wished to stay was too much for him.

He stepped to her and, gripping her chin, tilted her mouth up to him. He brushed his lips to hers and felt her shiver. How sweet she tasted. He pressed his mouth more fully upon her. She responded and tasted equally of him. Her tongue slipped passed his lips, impudently darting into his mouth at first, then seeking his tongue with increasing aggression. She grabbed his shirtfront and pulled him closer. He worked his mouth over her, and she him.

Her hands undid his breeches, and this time he did not stop her. She ran her hand along his length. Lowering her head, she licked at his cock, causing the blood to roil in his sac. She took his shaft into her mouth.

The Lord have mercy. Little wonder it had not taken Jonathan long to spend. Her hot, wet mouth felt wondrous. He threaded his fingers into her damp hair. She moved up and down his cock, taking him in so deep her lips touched the hair at his pelvis. He looked heavenward, glorying in her skills. She kept a steady pace, never once relinquishing the suction she had upon him. The head of his cock grazed the back of her throat over and over and over.

He moaned, feeling his climax approaching. His muscles tensed. She reached for his scrotum and tugged at his balls as she sucked him hard, pulling the seed from him. His hand tightened in her hair, and his hips bucked against her. Head back, he roared his release. She sputtered a little but drank of his seed until he had pumped the last of it down her throat.

"Glorious," he acknowledged as he pulled his softened cock from her mouth.

He kissed her and tasted the tangy flavor of his own seed. He pushed her down into the bed and lay atop her, planting kisses upon her neck. She undid the buttons of his shirt and caressed the planes of his chest, his ribs, his back. When she cupped his buttocks, he felt himself hardening again. He pushed a breast up to his mouth and sucked at her nipple. She arched under him. He fondled the nipple with his tongue until she bucked against him, desiring him to touch her quim. Taking his cock in hand, he rubbed her folds and felt the moisture of her heat.

"Ah," she breathed when he slipped inside of her.

"Surely Tremayne cannot pleasure you as well," he growled low into her ear.

He sank himself further into her.

"Never," she admitted.

He rolled his hips. "Then why do you trifle with a boy such as he? Does the Lady Debarlow not deserve a man?"

She responded with a growl of her own. "Are you jealous, Sir?"

He was. He wanted the Baroness for himself.

"Your attention to him is baffling," he replied. "A woman like you cannot be satisfied by the likes of Tremayne."

"He satisfies another desire of mine."

"What manner of desire?"

She did not answer but moved her hips in time to him.

"You have taken pity upon him?" he pursued.

"Hah. Hardly."

He pulled back to look her in the eyes. "You are contemptuous of him. Why bind yourself to him in matrimony if you disapprove of him?"

When at first she did not answer, he slid his hand between them to molest her clit.

"I abhor him," she revealed.

Her reply only confused him more.

"You enjoy suffering," he suggested, hoping to coax more revelations through his caresses. "No other reasoning can explain your situation if you detest him."

She shook her head.

"Then why marry the Viscount?"

Saying nothing, she ground her hips against him. He thrust into her, making her groan and cling tightly to him.

"Why marry Tremyane?" he repeated.

She grasped at his cock with her cunnie and bucked against him when he slowed.

"Why?" he questioned again.

She thrust her pelvis at his, but he remained motionless. He withdrew his cock.

She sighed in exasperation. "Because I abhor his father more."

He pushed his cock into her, and began a steady pounding of her cunnie. She wanted revenge, he realized. He knew well that nothing would distress the Earl more. Without knowing more, he found himself sympathetic to her purpose. As she wrapped her legs about him, his thoughts took lesser priority to the sensations engulfing his loins. He turned his attention to making her spend. He shoved himself deep into her, eliciting a cry. Their bodies undulated against each other, rocking the bed beneath them. She had not a frail body, and he shoved himself hard against her. They bucked in unison and when her release began to shake through her body, he could no longer hold back his own climax. He spent inside of her, roaring and grinding the last of his seed into her cunnie before collapsing on top of her.

Never had a climax felt so gratifying, and Montague idly wondered if her confidence had aught to do with his sense of fulfillment. He kissed her lightly upon the neck. As much as he enjoyed feeling her beneath him, her pointed nipples digging into his chest, he wanted to hold her. Rolling to her side, he pulled her into his arms. The scent of their desire still clung to the air, and he took a contented breath. He felt tired and invigorated all at once.

She nestled into his embrace and, of a sudden, he felt *exceptional* and wanted the sensation to last forever. He dreaded the truth of the matter: that the feelings were the beginnings of love.

* * * * *

Abbey opened her eyes to see Montague sitting at the edge of the bed, dressed and shaved, staring upon her. She wondered that he could be up this early in the morning when they had spent the better part of the night making love not once or twice, but thrice. The fire of their lust seemed to burn even in their sleep such that she felt no rest. But she had relished every second. He had caressed her with surprising tenderness and bucked against her with such passion that she felt quite *exceptional*. She could see—jealously—how the women of Bath fell to his charms in the bed chamber.

He smiled at her, turning the jealousy into hope that perhaps he did consider her special. He held up a basket.

"I had Jonathan prepare a picnic that we might have breakfast overlooking the hills," he said with almost boyish excitement.

Relieved that she was not being sent home yet, she returned his smile. With his assistance, she dressed in her chemise and stays. After he had laced her back, he wrapped his arms around her waist and nuzzled her neck.

"Hmmm, I've a mind to undo what I have just done," he grumbled.

She turned around in his arms and circled her arms around his neck. "Why undo? I've no chastity belt about me."

He grabbed her thighs and lifted her up. She wrapped her legs about his hips. He backed her against the bedpost. She felt wet between the legs already. They kissed as he ground his pelvis into her. She gathered the skirt of her chemise about her loins. Holding her up with one arm, he undid his breeches with his other hand. She settled onto his cock and playfully bit at his ear. Once more the chamber was filled with the sound of their rutting and the fulfillment of a need as old as Eve.

"Do you entertain such ardor with all the women you seduce?" she asked when he had set her back on her feet.

"Not half," he replied.

She hoped it to be true. They finished her toilette and ventured out into the morning. He led her behind the dwelling and up a knoll overlooking hills covered in heather. She gasped at the plethora of purple blooms extending before her like an endless sea.

Montague had spread a blanket and began unpacking their picnic.

"The coffee would have been cold, but I have a bottle of *Moët et Chandon*," he said as he poured her a glass of the sparkling wine.

"A most breathtaking view," she said as she accepted the glass from him.

"As a boy, I would climb that tree behind us, perch myself upon a branch, and eat my caramels to this vista."

"I should have loved to spend a childhood growing up upon such lands."

He nodded. "I have always felt at peace here in Chelton."

She remembered his response to her earlier question about the property but decided not to bring up a topic that might prove awkward.

"You must have been a naughty boy," she implicated instead.

"My lady," he responded in shocked dismay. "What have I done to have given you such an impression?"

She laughed.

"And were you not a naughty little girl?"

She raised her chin, but her eyes twinkled. "I was a perfectly behaved little girl with much joy in my heart."

Her final words faltered a little upon her tongue.

"And now?" he questioned as he sliced an apple.

"It were much more fun to misbehave."

"And the joy?" he persisted.

She plucked a grape from its stem. "Joy is reserved for the young and innocent."

"When did my lady lose her innocence?"

She thought about the confidence she had already revealed to him. "When I was four and ten. At the hand of the Earl of Frotham."

He choked on his apple. "Did he ravish you?"

"Nay."

He looked relieved. The redness in his face receded. "Then how?"

"As he is a friend of yours—"

"He is no friend of mine," he assured her. "I suspect he disdains me."

"But you are a friend of Richard Henry. They are as tight as peas in a pod."

"Circumstances force me not to scorn their company, but an you are successful in your vengeance upon him, Frotham will receive no sympathy from me."

Convinced of his sincerity, she elaborated. "He was my mother's lover. My father had passed away when I was young. My mother was a beauty and attracted the attentions of the Earl, though she could have selected from a number of eager suitors. She fell in love with Frotham."

She looked over the hills, but this time she did not see the blooms. She saw only her mother's frail body, the sores upon her from laying days in a bed.

"He had promised to wed her," she continued, "but was convinced by his father to pursue the riches of the New World. When he had returned to England, he wrote that he would come see her soon. My mother made herself ill waiting for him. I had attempted to see him, to let him know that my mother was not well. 1 was still a child then and had not the proper appreciation of our differences. As you know, my family was considered far too *bourgeois* for the likes of a Frotham.

"And then we had word of his engagement to the daughter of a nobleman. He ceased writing to my mother. She died of a broken heart. Only…"

Tears that had been dry for years suddenly formed in her eyes. "Only Fate was Unkind. I would she had thrown herself into the sea that Death might have taken her sooner. Instead, Death took her little by little. For a sixmonth, I watched her waste away. I changed her linens. I fed her. I sang to her though it was as if I no longer existed for her. Though I was her only child.

"I sent letters to Frotham begging him to see her, begging him to send money for a doctor. Until at last, I prayed for Death. I begged for Death to take her. She had ceased to take any food, but I could—I could hear her stomach growling with hunger."

Her words turned into a sob. When Montague wrapped his arms about her, he unleashed a dam. The tears poured from her eyes. Turning into his shoulder, she succumbed to the cries that had welled inside of her for years. She thought she had turned her pain into a drive for revenge upon the man who had wronged her, but her aim had only masked the pain. And yet, despite the anguish and the agony, she found relief in speaking her memories and comfort in his embrace. In contrast to the long and solitary days and the long and solitary nights spent at her mother's bedside, she was not now alone.

Montague said nothing but put a hand to her head as if to shield her from the menace in the world. When the fiercest of her sobs had subsided, she lay with her head against his chest. She heard the beating of his heart, a strong and comforting rhythm. And in that moment, she surrendered herself wholly to him.

CHAPTER EIGHTEEN

A S SHE TOLD HER story, Montague could hear the breaking of her heart and would have killed the Earl if he had thought it would do any good. He now admired Abigail Debarlow even more. She had planned the perfect and poetic revenge. He did not believe that the success of her vengeance would bring her peace, but it could do no damage.

Except to him. If he did not fulfill his end of the bargain, Chelton would be lost to him.

He held her closer. "Your fury with Frotham—with the male sex— is most justified."

"I am not cross at all men," she objected as she looked up at him.

He looked down at her and brushed away a tendril of her hair that threatened to fall in front of her eyes. "Are you not?"

She glanced away. "Perhaps a little."

"Little wonder you are also disillusioned with love."

"I had thought that love, at least between a mother and child, would always be pure. But for my mother, the will to live *for her child* was eclipsed by the *loss of a man*."

He wondered if the true source of her bitterness might not be her own mother and not Frotham, though the living provided an easier target for vengeance than the dead. Something in the way the Earl had spoken gave Montague the suspicion that, odious as Frotham was, he might have loved Abigail's mother in return.

"Did your desire for vengeance inspire you to aspire to polite society then?" he asked.

"Though I had not the full beauty of my mother, I knew I possessed enough to attract men of any class. I became the mistress to one when I was seven and ten years of age. I found it an easy matter to move progressively from one to another."

"Until you finally landed upon the Baron Debarlow."

"You would not believe that I did not have him in my sights. I was a patron of *Madame Botreaux* and a submissive to a man who enjoyed the pleasures of a man as well as a woman. Debarlow was his other submissive. As I was intimate with him in *The Cavern*, I knew him to possess a scar upon his right forearm, the result of a rapier duel.

"We happened to be at a garden party. A lady dropped her fan into the fountain. He rolled up his sleeve to retrieve it for her, and I saw the scar. I know your thoughts: you perceive that I had blackmailed him. I did confront him in private, but he could have just as easily have blackmailed me. We became friends. Marriage was his idea. It was quite convenient for him, you see. He would not have to hide his visits to *Madame Botreaux's* with me as his wife. I would attain the status I had sought. Marriage was mutually beneficial."

Part of him did not wish to know too much about her relationship with the Baron, but he had to ask, "You were not in love with him then?"

"I bore him much affection, but he loved our master at the time. I admired him for his courage in marrying me. It was from him that I learned to live mine own life and polite society be damned."

He tilted her chin up with his knuckle. "You are a marvelous woman, Lady Debarlow."

He kissed her mouth, her nose, her forehead. He tasted the salt on her cheeks left by her tears and once more claimed the softness of her lips. But kissing her was no easy matter for he instantly felt a stronger desire to take her. She responded by unbuttoning her caraco. He kissed the top of her bosom, grasped a breast in his hand, sinking his fingers into the pliable flesh. He leaned her into the ground and covered her with his weight.

She seemed to recall something. "Tell me, how did you know I was a patron of *Madame Botreaux*?"

"I recognized your snuffbox."

He did not reveal that he was first informed by Jonathan.

"Ah."

"I shall forever be grateful to that little snuffbox."

Her eyes shone brightly, glimmering with the last of her tears. "And I."

After he had thrown her skirts above her waist and licked her cunnie until she squealed with delight and her cries had sent the birds from the trees, he rolled her on top of him. She rode his rigid cock as skillfully as she rode her horse. After they had both spent, they finished their picnic. He took her on a walk of the grounds at Chelton. Having her upon his arm, laughing and teasing him as he described moments from his childhood, was as delightful as fucking her over the back of a chair. He wished that they could remain forever at Chelton.

But Chelton would not be his to have if he did not achieve his objective. He had seduced the Baroness, had taken her to his bed, but would this prove sufficient for Frotham? His success, moreover, would be her failure. He would have denied her the vengeance she had sought.

"Were you truly *en route* to Gretna Green with Tremayne?" he asked as they passed beneath a large willow tree.

"I was."

"You would have married him?"

"Aye."

"You deserve better, Abbey."

She waved a dismissive hand. "He would be a husband in name only. Once he was bound to me, I would be free to entertain any man I wished."

"Would that not upset Charles?"

She shrugged. "He could accuse me of *crim con* and seek a divorce, but the dye of scandal would be cast."

"And you think, after you have avenged the death of your mother, that you would be contented?"

"I think it would."

He decided not to dispute her supposition. Playfully, he kissed her hand. "Do you intend to take many lovers when you are a married woman?"

She grinned at him. "Would you dare to be my paramour?"

"And make a cuckold of poor Charles?"

"There is no 'poor Charles.' The apple does not fall far from the tree."

He raised his brows but did not doubt her assertion. Making a cuckold of Charles was not a true concern of his. He had cuckolded enough husbands in his lifetime. But for once, he thought he might prefer to be the husband instead of the paramour.

"And if you should be unable to marry Charles?" he asked.

Her face darkened a little. "Yes, you have set back my plans."

"Would you be much saddened?"

She became silent in thought. "Would I have you to console me?"

He allowed her to artfully dodge his question. He had hoped that she might reconsider her plans to marry Charles, but he would not push the subject overly much with her.

"But of course," he replied as he turned up her wrist and touched his lips there.

The light kiss sent butterflies through her, and she knew it would not be long before time would find them tumbling against each other upon the ground.

"Have you many other women to console back in Bath?" she asked as she played with the buttons upon his coat, hoping his answer would not rattle her too much.

He watched as she undid his buttons. "None."

"Because you are the perpetrator?"

"To be honest, in some instances."

"Is that why you have come to London? To escape the hearts you had broken?"

"I would be presumptuous to assert I was of such significance in a woman's life as to have had such an impact upon her heart. I have slighted many a vanity, to be sure. As for London, I had not been to the

City in some time. And an unexpected business proposition compelled me to stay."

She pushed his coat off his shoulders. He slid his arms out.

"It were damnably unfair that men should have such ease undressing," she murmured, pressing a hot kiss to his throat.

"I am partial to the challenges of a lady's attire."

Her caraco was unbuttoned and he brushed his fingers over the bare skin above her décolletage. His touch ignited her desire.

"No doubt you are much practiced in the task."

"Perhaps, but I may be outmatched in present company."

She reached between his legs and grabbed his sac. He grunted, cupped her face with both hands, and devoured her mouth. She would have been content to kiss him for hours were it not for the yearning ache between her thighs. He whipped her around and began removing her garments one by one, kissing and caressing every inch of skin that he laid bare until she had only her stockings and shoes. She wiggled her rump against his crotch as his arms circled around her. He kneaded her breasts and pinched her nipples.

"Place your hands upon the tree," he instructed. He broke off a branch and, using it as a switch, laid it upon her arse.

"Thank you, Sir," she responded instantly and arched her derriere for him.

He pushed her feet wider apart and lashed upwards between her legs at her cunnie. She gasped at the pain and felt her juices flowing.

"Thank you, Sir."

He rubbed the switch along her clit. She moaned.

"Take me, Sir."

He obliged and, situating himself behind her, slid his cock into her. She marveled at how he filled her despite the many times he had already entered. Using the tree as leverage, she pushed her rump into his pelvis. He bucked against her with enough force that, had her hand slipped, she would have found her face planted against the tree. She cried out happily. Lessening the force of his thrust, he told her to pleasure herself. She put a hand between her thighs and caressed her mons. She did not require long to ascend her peak.

Pulling out of her, he grabbed his coat and spread it upon the ground for her. Her thighs fell to the sides for him. He threw her legs over his shoulders and penetrated her hard, burying his pole to the hilt in her now sodden cunnie. Her previous climax had barely subsided when she felt another looming. Their bodies pumped vigorously against one another. They panted in rhythm. She knew she would never know a better partner in this carnal dance as the most beautiful sensations burst from between her legs, sending shudders to the points of her fingers and toes. Montague came almost in unison, a conclusion as satisfying as her own.

He wrapped his coat about her and held her as she rested her eyes. They napped upon the grass until a breeze began to entice little bumps upon her skin.

"I wonder that you ever wish to leave Chelton," she remarked as he assisted in redressing her.

"The memories here are not all happy ones," he conceded. "My mother was never entirely fond of the place. My father incurred a great amount of debt as a result of this estate. Nevertheless, I am loathe to part with it."

She took in a deep breath of the heather-scented air. Here she felt the promise of a tranquility she had not known in some time.

"That were quite understandable. One could be at peace here."

He turned her to him with surprising emotion. "Could you envision happiness here?"

"I—I don't know," she stammered. "I think I have far too much bitterness in my soul to know true happiness."

"And you think achieving vengeance upon Frotham will alleviate your bitterness?"

She looked down at the ground, envisioning the look of consternation upon the Earl, imagining the torment he would feel, visualizing a life married to Charles or the spectacle of divorce.

"If it would, I wish you much success in your endeavor," Montague added. "Indeed, I admire your perseverance. You have a purpose.

Something I have lacked in my life. But it would be tragic if your efforts did not provide you the relief you seek."

And kept her from the promise of something better, she realized. All of a sudden, she was overcome with sadness. She no longer found her revenge exalting. A tear slipped down her cheek.

He brushed her tear away with his thumb and kissed the top of the head. "We are neither of us are such saints that we should be blessed with all that the heavens may offer; but neither are we so wretched that we should be denied all happiness. Perhaps if we were to allow ourselves some amount of joy, together we can be better than we are."

More tears pressed themselves to her eyes—tears of relief and hope. She looked up at him and nodded. He folded his arms about her and pulled her into his chest. She clung to the lapels of his coat and let out a shaky breath.

* * * * *

The carriage bounced erratically upon the dirt road, but with the Baroness in his arms, Montague no longer minded the journey. They had both wanted to stay at Chelton, but it would not do for the Baroness Debarlow to be missing for much longer. The return to London, however, did not dim his excitement. Abbey had decided to relinquish the Viscount of her own accord, freeing him from his dilemma. He had deliberated in his mind over and over how he ought to proceed with her, given his arrangement with the Earl. He fell upon one overarching realization: he wanted Abbey for himself. If she renounced Tremayne, he could claim his payment from the Earl. With Chelton secured, he could turn his attentions to wooing Lady Debarlow in earnest.

Providence had indeed smiled upon him. Nothing could prevent him from claiming the Baroness as his.

CHAPTER NINETEEN

EVALINE PRESSED HER EAR carefully to the door of her father's study. Mr. Henry had warned her to stay her distance from the likes of Montague Edwards. She would have thought Mr. Henry to be merely overly protecting of her, and she knew full well the reputation Edwards had in Bath, but the vitriol in his tone made her suspect something else was afoot. Had Mr. Henry not introduced Edwards as a cousin though the two bore not the slightest resemblance? Furthermore, she failed to understand why her father would keep Edwards' company if the latter was such a reprobate.

"I had saved your son from running off to Gretna Green with Lady Debarlow," Edwards was saying.

Gretna Green? That foolish brother of hers! It was not indecent enough for him to be courting her but he must elope with her to boot? Her heart warmed with gratitude towards Edwards. Was that why her father had called upon him?

"But have you seduced the Baroness enough?" her father questioned. "Who is to say that they will not make another attempt at Gretna Green?"

"Have you spoken with your son?"

"No, no, it were better he presume I knew nothing or he might be even more driven to keep his actions secret."

"He would tell you the Baroness has foresworn his attentions."

"You do not know the Baroness as I do. She can be extremely deceptive and wily. I will not be comforted till Charles has agreed to marry Elisabeth."

"Our arrangement was for me to seduce the Lady Debarlow, not to convince your son to marry Miss Worsely."

"He will if he has lost all hope of reconciling with the Baroness."

Silence fell. Evaline imagined Edwards to be seething for his tone had grown increasingly angry. Now her father's association with the rake made sense. But how inconsiderate of her father to demand more of the man! Her stomach churned with jealousy. The Baroness had already had her share of men, including her brother, and would add Edwards to her growing list?

"I will require more time then," Edwards said at last, "and will have it in writing."

"Done. I will have papers sent to you on the morrow."

Evaline stumbled away from the door upon hearing footsteps approach, but Edwards stormed from the room without noticing her. He headed outside to await his horse. She followed him outside.

"Mr. Edwards!" she greeted. "I thought I beheld you from upstairs. Have you taken yourself to Ranalegh Gardens as I had advised?"

"Admittedly, I have not," he replied coolly with a bow.

It was clear his mind was elsewhere. On the Baroness no doubt. How she wished her father were not so stubborn! This was all Charles' doing!

"There is to be a new comedy at the Theatre Royal. I shall be in attendance Saturday. Perhaps if you are not otherwise engaged—"

He adjusted his gloves. "I doubt I shall be at liberty to attend."

Evaline bit her lower lip, feeling the desperation rise in her throat. "Then perhaps you will visit Vauxhall? Many a chaperone has been lost in its gardens."

He turned to look at her. At last!

"Lady Evalina?"

She lowered her lashes "I am young but not so naïve as one might think. My position demands a certain decorum."

She dropped her voice. "But a more vibrant passion burns within me. I yearn to know—"

"Lady Evalina, your father would have me killed were I to ruin you."

"He pays me no heed as his attentions are fixed upon my brother. I presume, also, that you are a man of great discretion."

"Lady Evalina, with your loveliness, you could tempt the saints."

Her heart soared at the compliment. She heard the footman come round with the horse and wished that she could have more time with Edwards. She watched as he mounted his horse.

He touched his hat to her. "But, alas, I am no saint."

He spurred his horse and departed. She felt hollow inside. How could he reject her with such ease? The cause must lie with his arrangement with the Earl. It were fruitless to talk to her father, but...

Turning on her heels, Evaline headed inside and to her chambers. She would draft a letter to the Baroness Debarlow.

* * * * *

"Your note had sent a dagger through my heart at first, but I could not believe you had meant it. And then to hear that you had been abducted by highwaymen—it was more than I could bear!"

Charles clasped Abbey to him, but she extricated herself from his awkward embrace.

"When I heard you were safely returned, I had to rush here to see for myself that you are safe and sound."

She went to the sideboard of her salon to pour herself a glass of port. She would not have the vengeance she had sought upon the Earl, but Libby would have hers.

"I have been near to Bedlam these past days," Charles lamented. "I could not sleep in wondering if you had come to harm."

"Did you attempt to find me?" she asked.

Charles stared blankly. "I thought you to have abandoned me. It was not until two days later that I heard from your servants that you were missing."

She thought wryly of the glove she had attempted to leave behind. Thank God she had not truly been abducted by highwaymen.

"Have you reconsidered your letter then?" he persisted. "We could leave for Gretna Green as early as tonight."

She sighed. "I meant every word, Charles. I am quite convinced that you and I are not suited."

He paled. "Not suited? Impossible!"

She sat down in her favorite wing-chair. "There is naught to recommend a match betwixt you and I."

"Is our mutual affection not enough? Our shared *interests?*"

"You would tire of me quickly. You may think that your title and family have no influence upon you, but they would eventually weigh upon you, and you would come to resent me."

Charles knelt before her. "I could never resent you! I would forever be happy to oblige you."

"Then oblige me now. Miss Worsely awaits your attention. She is young and beautiful. She comes from a prestigious family."

She could hardly believe that she was encouraging that which would make Frotham happy, but it mattered less now.

Charles scowled. "Elisabeth is a child!"

"No more than you, m'dear."

"But—but our disparity in years did not hinder you before."

"I have come to my senses or my tendencies to the caprice with regards to my lovers has prevailed."

Charles grew red of face, not unlike his father. "Lovers? Have you another lover?"

"That has no bearing upon my decision—"

"Who is he? Another patron of *Madame Botreaux?*"

She stared him in the eyes and said in her most imposing tone. "I will not marry you, Charles."

He rose to his feet. Various hues flashed through his physiognomy. "You will regret your decision, Abbey. I could have offered you more than any other man. You will wish you had not cast me aside."

He whirled angrily upon his heels. She wondered what rash intentions he had, but Charles was no longer her concern. Settling into her seat, she finished her wine when her butler entered.

"A letter came by messenger for you," he said.

She took the letter from the tray, wondering if it might be from Montague Edwards. She could hardly wait to see him once more.

Putting aside her glass, she eagerly opened the letter. At once she saw, however, that the penmanship was that of a woman.

"Abbey, what is this about your being abducted?" Constance swept into the room. "And how is it I have not learned of this before? My dear, you are pale as a ghost."

The letter blurred before Abbey's gaze as she handed it to Constance, but the contents of the letter haunted her mind.

Constance scanned the letter. "Shocking! I can hardly believe that Frotham would deign to make such a proposal."

"I believe it," Abbey replied. "The Earldom is everything to him. As for Edwards…"

Constance sank into the settee opposite her friend. Abbey knit her brows. Her friend was not leaping to his defense?

"What intelligence have you?" she asked.

Constance took a deep breath. "I had thought you and Mr. Edwards to have formed a *bond* of sorts. Wanting to know more about him, I elicited all that I could from his friend Mr. Holmes. I plied the man with the best wine from my brother's cellar and learned that Edwards is short of funds. Apparently he has outstanding notes upon some property of his. He came to London to find a wife of means."

Abbey recalled the references to Chelton by Montague himself: the insecurity of his ownership, the debt incurred by his father, his desire to retain Chelton.

The air about her seemed to thin. How fortunate for Montague. If he had been successful in becoming her paramour, she would certainly qualify as a woman of means. But with the Earl's proposition, he had only to seduce her away from Tremayne.

"Dearest…" Constance murmured. "I regret my hand in introducing you to that loathsome Edwards. What a poor friend am I!"

"You could not have known," Abbey consoled.

"What a relief that you a woman of singular mind and will simply move onto the next man."

"Yes, one lover is as good as the next."

But the words rang hollow to her own ears. It would have been a simple matter, as Constance put it, had she not fallen in love with the man.

CHAPTER TWENTY

LATIMER CLAPPED MONTAGUE on the back as he threw the *Times* onto the table of the coffee-house. "Well done, Edwards! The Earl is sure to reward you now."

Edwards looked at the assertion in the paper that the banns for the Viscount Tremayne and Miss Elisabeth Worsely would soon be read.

Montague gave his friend a half smile. The news was delightful, but his victory would not be complete without the Baroness. Strangely, she had taken herself from town without word to him. He could only speculate that she wanted no part of all the gossip that was sure to fly about her and Tremayne. There would be many who would openly snicker before her. Tremayne was already spreading the falsehood that he had tired of the Baroness.

The play that Lady Evalina had suggested was still playing at the Royal a fortnight later, and Montague decided it might prove an effective distraction. If he did not fill his time, he found himself dwelling on Abbey—longing for her company and craving her body. The atmosphere at the theatre was boisterous that evening with a full house. He observed that Tremayne was in attendance, as was Miss Worsely. The former was not particularly attentive to his impending fiancée, and the latter appeared bored by her company.

"Odd's bodkins, is that not the Baroness Debarlow?" Latimer asked after he and Montague had taken their seats.

Montague followed the gaze of his friend up to a box in the third level. His heart skipped a beat. It was Abbey. She looked regal in her gown of ivory and gold damask. Had she been in London long?

He looked to Tremayne and saw that the Viscount, too, had noticed her presence. Montague could hardly wait for intermission and was out of his seat the instant the first act drew to an end. He made his way to the third level and saw that Abbey had emerged from her box and was accepting a cup of confections from Lady Constance. The Viscount and Miss Worsely, whose box was on the same level, passed at that moment. The Viscount bumped the arm of the Baroness as he walked by. The lemon drops spilled onto her, and she dropped her opera glasses. Montague would have collared the Viscount, but too many people stood betwixt him and Treymane. Instead, he quickly made his way to the Baroness.

"Insolent little wretch," Lady Constance was mumbling.

Montague picked up the glasses and returned them to Abbey. She started upon seeing him, and he was unsure of the expression upon her face. If he were unprejudiced, he would have thought that she was not pleased to see him. Lady Constance, too, seemed tentative.

"Lady Debarlow, Lady Constance," he bowed.

"Mr. Edwards," Abbey returned.

There was no mistaking the coolness in her tone. Something was amiss.

"Might I have a word with her ladyship?" he asked.

Lady Constance looked at her friend, who nodded.

"I shall not be long—or far," Lady Constance said as she sauntered away.

He followed Abbey into her box.

"It has been too long," he said as he kissed her hand. "I would take you into my arms if there were not a hundred pair of eyes present."

She withdrew her hand from his. "What is it you wished to speak to me of, Mr. Edwards?"

The formality of her tone struck him as odd since no one was within earshot.

"Why did you not inform me when you had left London? Or that you had returned."

"Because you are not my keeper, Mr. Edwards."

He did not like the indifference he heard.

"But—"

"Is your business in London not concluded?"

He raised his brows curiously.

"Tremayne is engaged to Worsely."

He felt the creeping of dread.

"You have accomplished what the Earl desired."

Time seemed to stop. Abbey knew. Somehow she knew of his arrangement with Frotham.

"How long have you known?" he asked quietly.

"What does it matter? I ought to thank you—or should I credit Frotham? I am relieved to be free of Tremayne. I had forgotten how *tedious* attaching myself to one man can be."

The sensation in his groin was not one that he welcomed this time. She reclined in her chair, stretching out her legs and propping her feet upon a footstool. She waved a can of large ostrich plumes in front of her.

"To placate my curiosity," she continued. "What was your reward?"

He frowned but did not wish to waver with timidity in his response. "Five and twenty thousand pounds."

"You command quite the sum, Mr. Edwards. You were wise to accept the offer from Frotham. I would not have paid any paramour of mine such monies."

It was rare in his life that he was struck dumb, but Montague could barely move. He would have gladly stood in the truth of what he had done and professed that, while he did require the funds, he had not expected to fall in love. And love her he did.

But judging from her disinterested expression, it mattered not. Her cynicism of the male sex was too great. Given his reputation, he was likely the last man of earth who could convince her otherwise. Perhaps the vulnerability that he had been privy to at Chelton, the hope and desire that he thought they two had shared, was but a moment in time. A passing dream.

"But I owe you much appreciation," she said.

He perked up, but his hopefulness was soon dashed.

"I see that my quest for revenge had consumed me overmuch. I am pleased to return to my old form. You and I are peas of a pod. We had a droll and amusing romp, did we not?"

Droll? Amusing? Was that how she viewed their time at Chelton together? Part of him wanted to sweep her into his arms and remind her of how she could not refuse him. He was sure he could reignite her passion given the chance.

But her next statement sent a chill that stayed his hand.

"I congratulate you and wish you well in your return to Bath—or Chelton."

She gave him her hand. He stared at it. He, Montague Edwards, was being dismissed. His mind still reeling from her words, he bowed wordlessly over her hand and rose to his feet. The blood had drained from his face. He had imagined that she had tender feelings for him. She had not promised herself to him, afterall. He pulled at his cravat and noticed that his heart was beating boldly—and painfully.

Pushing aside the curtain and exiting her box, he nearly collided with Lady Constance.

"I beg your pardon," he mumbled.

She looked at him in surprise, but then averted her gaze. He would find no champion in her. He thought of all the possible women who might have mistaken his actions for affection. He had glibly gone from one woman to the next without much consideration for how they might have felt. The fortune he thought Fate had bestowed upon him was a falsehood for he had finally met his match in the Baroness Debarlow.

CHAPTER TWENTY-ONE

Six Months Later—MONTAGUE FINISHED OFF the last of the
wine and shrugged into his scarlet coat. He tossed the serving
wench at the tavern a half penny and assisted his friend to his
feet. Latimer stumbled a bit, then looked Montague from head to foot.

"Must admit you cut a dapper figure in redcoat, Edwards," Latimer
slurred as he flecked at the gold epaulets. "Will you not be stinkin' hot
in such a garb?"

Montague had heard the climate in India could melt a man, but
when he had purchased a commission in His Majesty's Army, he had
not expected that his regiment would be called to duty a world away.
But he welcomed the change as an opportunity to put distance to his
memories of *her*.

"You shall miss England—even the damnable weather here,"
Latimer added as he allowed Montague to guide him out the tavern. He
put a hand to his head. "I would rise and see you off with your regiment
tomorrow, but I suspect I'll have a ghastly headache in the morning."

"I shall write you often enough," replied Montague as he hailed a
chair and assisted his friend into it.

Latimer nodded. "You must. I shall die of boredom an' you do not.
Neither Bath nor London will be half as interesting without your
presence. *Bon voyage*, my friend."

Montague watched the chair disappear into the night. He would
miss Latimer. And England. But he was reminded of Abbey too much
here. He thought about the pretty tavern wench he had just left and
contemplated having one final tumble with an Englishwoman before

sailing off tomorrow, but the urge rang hollow nowadays. He pulled out his snuffbox instead and was about to take a pinch when something was thrown over his head—a sack perhaps—and blinded him. Hands grabbed at his arms. He elbowed one of his assailants, but there must have been two of them. They pinioned his arms and tied his wrists. Before he could cry out, he was thrown onto the floor of a vehicle. He kicked at them, but the door was slammed. He heard the crack of a whip, and the vehicle lurched forward. He was in a carriage. But why?

He sat himself up and listened for other occupants of the vehicle. He heard a rustle, but with the sack over his head, he could see nothing. Nonetheless, he was sure he was not alone.

"What manner of prank is this?" he demanded as he considered which of his fellow officers might be involved.

"This be no trick but vengeance."

He recognized the woman's voice!

"Abbey?"

The sack was pulled from his head.

"Why, Mr. Edwards," she noted, "I thought you disdained powder."

Without light, he saw only shadows in the dim light of the stars. He drank in her silhouette.

"It is required of officers," he replied, his heart racing. What did she intend with him?

"Are you not pleased to see me?"

Elated would have been a fitting word. Not a day went by and he did not think of her.

"If I am remiss in courtesies, it is merely because I must prepare to set sail tomorrow with my regiment."

"I know. To India."

"It would not go well with me if I failed to report for duty."

"Indeed."

He struggled with his binds, but they were steadfast. How long did she intend to keep him?

"Why India?" she asked.

"There appears to be some unrest threatening the operations of the East India Company."

"Why the army?" she rephrased. "You do not strike me as the sort to pursue such a career."

"I was in search of a purpose, my lady," he answered honestly. "The army be a fitting place for a man such as myself with no ties nor loved ones."

"There is no one you love here in England?"

He paused. "No one who would miss me."

"Are you quite sure?"

What a strange question. What did she mean by it? How he wished there was light that he might see her face! Although he had sought to push away memories of her, he now wanted one last chance to look upon her.

"My lady?"

"If there should be the prospect of one who would…?"

Her voice cracked with emotion. His heart beat in his ears.

"If it be the Lady Debarlow—but I dare not hope," he responded, stunned at the turn of events, but determined to voice that which he did not in their last encounter.

"I saw that Chelton was for sale by Mr. Richard Henry," she said. "I learned that he held the notes, secured by Chelton, in the amount of five and ten thousand pounds. Constance confirmed with Mr. Holmes that you had not accepted your payment from Frotham. Consequently, Chelton was forfeited to Mr. Henry."

"I was paid an advance of five thousand pounds."

"But you gave up Chelton."

"I did not want Frotham's money."

"Why?"

"To my chagrin, Lady Debarlow, I grew a conscience of late. It were damned inconvenient, really."

She let out a shaky laugh. He decided to show his cards for he had nothing to gain from keeping mum. "Moreover, Chelton held too many memories of you."

There was silence, and he could not be sure how she received this revelation. Overcome with feeling, he looked down to gather himself.

"Then you have no need to set foot upon Chelton?" she inquired at last.

"I do not," he replied firmly.

"A pity. For we are headed there."

He looked at her sharply. To Chelton? If the tide went out early, they would not return in time for him to be aboard the ship.

"It a beautiful property and should not reside with just anyone," she said, "so I purchased it from Mr. Henry. He would not sell it to me at first, but in the end, he was persuaded, as he has a son of his own not far in age from Tremayne…"

He was still reeling from the fact that she had purchased Chelton when she slid off her seat and straddled his legs upon the carriage floor.

"And its dungeons fit quite well into my plans for revenge," she finished.

He could feel her breath upon his face. Her lips were inches from his.

"A rather extravagant revenge," he commented.

"And penance. I was mistaken and wrong to have cast you aside. I only did so because…because I thought you did not care for me."

He could hardly breathe from the emotions waving over him. The pureness of the joy had him nearly mute once more. Her eyes shined in the darkness with what might have been tears. His muscles tensed from the desire to clasp her to his bosom.

"Abbey…would it offend my lady if I were to declare my love for you?"

She brushed her lips lightly over his. "Only an' you did not take me as you did once before."

He felt his cock lengthen. "Then unbind me now, Baroness."

She reached around him and loosened the rope at his wrists. He cupped her face and pressed his lips to hers with the intention of never letting her go.

THE END

CAVERN OF PLEASURE SERIES

OTHER WORKS BY EM BROWN

Cavern of Pleasure Series
Mastering the Marchioness
Conquering the Countess
Binding the Baroness
Lord Barclay's Seduction

Red Chrysanthemum Stories
Master vs. Mistress
Master vs. Mistress: The Challenge Continues
Seducing the Master
Taking the Temptress
Master vs. Temptress: The Final Submission
A Wedding Night Submission
Punishing Miss Primrose, Parts I - XX

Chateau Debauchery Series
Submitting to the Rake
Submitting to Lord Rockwell
Submitting to His Lordship
Submitting to the Baron
Submitting to the Marquess
Submitting for Christmas

Other Stories
Claiming a Pirate